Readers love *Unicorn Tracks*
by JULIA EMBER

"I greatly enjoyed *Unicorn Tracks*, and consider it a masterpiece all on it's own."
—The Book Deviant

"A deep and beautiful world… Characters you can root for."
—Binge On Books

"*Unicorn Tracks* is an incredibly fresh story, with a seldom before seen setting that you don't want to miss."
—The Bookavid

"This book was something else, it was amazing."
—Book Babbles and Blues

By JULIA EMBER

The Tiger's Watch
Unicorn Tracks

Published by HARMONY INK PRESS
www.harmonyinkpress.com

Julia Ember

The Tiger's Watch

Harmony Ink

Published by

HARMONY INK PRESS

5032 Capital Circle SW, Suite 2, PMB# 279, Tallahassee, FL 32305-7886 USA
publisher@harmonyinkpress.com • harmonyinkpress.com

The Tiger's Watch
© 2017 Julia Ember.

Cover Art
© 2017 Meghan Moss.
http://meaghz.deviantart.com/gallery/
Cover content is for illustrative purposes only and any person depicted on the cover is a model.
Map Art
© 2017 Beth at https://www.fiverr.com/bethips.

ISBN: 978-1-63533-485-2
Digital ISBN: 978-1-63533-486-9
Library of Congress Control Number: 2017903382
Published August 2017
v. 1.0

Printed in the United States of America
(∞)
This paper meets the requirements of
ANSI/NISO Z39.48-1992 (Permanence of Paper).

For my Dad: Thank you for letting me experience 99 and 100 with you, and for the lifelong wanderlust you've inspired.

★Achinsk

KYZYL

Nor'sk•

Nova Zem Forest

•Raza

Pakke Lake

Valley of a
Thousand Temples

★Jakar

✕Mines

Kun Long
Forest

River Doma

Trongsa•

•Mada Htet

•Bagoon

Khaling Mountains

MYEIK

★Yango

Mines✕

•Thiya

Mines✕

✕Mines

Mines✕

Pyay•

Mines✕

Mines✕

•Myede

Min
Eta

Silay
Lake

•Namsang

Lingzhi Sea

bethips 2016

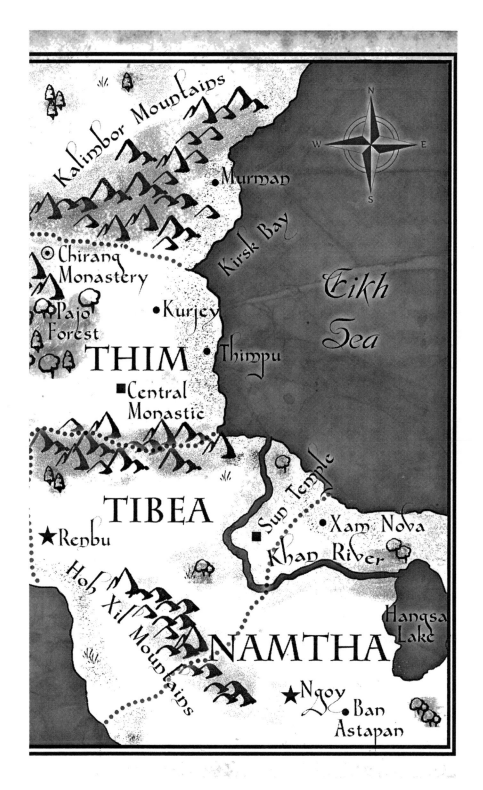

CHAPTER 1

WHILE THE capitol burned in a smoky hailstorm of tar and arrows, we escaped by elephant to the Chirang monastery. The elephant struggled to keep his balance on the slick, frozen ground as Pharo clicked his tongue to urge him forward. I rode behind the beast's ears, both arms wrapped around Kalx's warm, limp body.

An arrow hissed past my ear. I nearly screamed, but Pharo's brown hand covered my mouth as he pushed me down onto the elephant's neck. The coarse hairs on the creature's nape stood up, sharp against my cheek. Another arrow flew over my head. The yellow feathers in its tail quivered as it embedded in a tree trunk just feet away.

The beast flattened his ears and charged through the graveyard of butchered trees that surrounded the city toward the remaining forest in front of us. Smoke rose like a paper screen at our backs. I tried to breathe in time with Kalx's steady, unconscious heartbeat to keep myself calm. Once we reached the trees, we could disappear into the mountains, but until then, we were exposed to the Myeik soldiers who guarded Jakar's outer wall.

Fear made bile churn in my empty stomach. If the army caught us, we'd die.

I tightened my hold around Kalx.

"Call Katala," Pharo hissed, his breath hot against my frozen skin. His muscular arms circled around my waist, enveloping Kalx and me together. "I'll brace you."

I bit my lip, considering. The elephant picked up speed, nearly throwing us backward. "What if you can't hold us? We'll all slip."

A bolt of fire pierced the dawn as a flaming arrow blasted through the sky like a falling star.

Pharo shook me. "We don't have time to argue. Just do it!"

I closed my eyes and searched for the thread of magical connection with the animal I'd trained alongside for the past seven years. I could sense her in the distance—poised and waiting, watching us. My body went rigid in Pharo's hold as my link to Katala solidified. Silver orbs formed in the air and hung around us. Then Katala's growl echoed through me. I felt ghost leaves brush my fingers as she crept through the foliage, her sharp eyes trained on an archer's gray mare. The soldier's yellow cloak was streaked with soot and ash. His fear made the air smell of musk. Katala crouched low, her muscles gathering beneath her as she prepared to pounce. Gasping, I broke our connection so I wouldn't have to watch the slaughter. She knew what needed to be done.

A moment later, a scream ripped through the smoky air. The sound curdled my blood like sour milk. Then with a final burst of speed, the elephant stampeded under the cover of the trees.

I exhaled slowly. Cold sweat dripped down my neck. Pharo unwrapped his arms and leaned back as the beast slowed to a trot.

"Do you think he was the only one following?" I asked.

Pharo shrugged. "I think however many there were, Katala will handle it."

I attempted a smile and reached for his hand, giving it a squeeze before wrapping both of my arms around Kalx again. Pharo was right; Katala had always surpassed any challenge thrown at her. And I didn't think the soldiers would try to follow us now. The forest scared the Myeik. Their country was all open plains and stretches of water. The trees hid traps and disguised beasts they didn't understand.

The elephant answered to our teacher, and he knew where to take us. We settled into silence, catching our breath and watching the path behind us with fear-sharpened eyes. I didn't know what to say to ease the tension, so I reclined atop the great lumbering beast and watched the sun rise above the snow-capped mountain peaks. I wanted to search out Katala again, to check on her, but if she was midfight, one second of distraction could get her killed. Kalx shivered in my hold, and I pulled my cloak tighter around him.

After an hour of silent travel, Pharo leaned across the elephant's back to speak, straining his voice over the moaning wind. He pointed to the chiseled, narrow ridge ahead of us. Years of blistering ice-wind had whittled the rocky mountain into the jagged shape of a tower. "We should be getting close. Mistress Lhamo said it was just below the castle peak."

His voice was cheerful, falsely light. I pushed my fingers deeper under Kalx's armpits to warm them and tried to ignore the wet cold seeping through my woolen cloak. "I need a bath."

Pharo laughed. He tapped the elephant's rump gently with his stick when the animal stopped to pull a pinecone from the tree above. "Do you think they even have hot water up here? Everything looks wet or frozen. What do they burn?"

I stuck my tongue out and caught a snowflake on the tip. The lone drop of water only teased my thirst. After weeks of siege, the rivers of the capitol had smelled of urine and decaying vegetables, too putrid to drink. I relished this first, fresh taste of the mountains. "After these last few weeks, I'll be glad to see clean water at all."

He clapped my shoulder, but I could feel his fingers shaking through his threadbare gloves. He turned and looked behind us as the elephant pushed through a barrier of sapling pines. "I hope the wind picks up. Those tracks are deep. I don't want to lead them straight to the monastery."

I nodded, and we went back to our silence.

When we cleared the thick trees and entered a canyon, my jaw dropped. Nested high in the rocks with sheer cliffs on three sides, the Chirang monastery reminded me of a giant bird of prey with its head folded under one wing. Its strong white outer walls were covered in lacy feathers of ice and snow. Flashes of orange turrets and golden temple domes peeked through the cracks in the walls, hinting at a whole world beyond. Needles of ice pelted my face as the wind grew stronger, but we'd been riding for hours, and by then I was almost too numb to feel them. Pharo let out a whoop of triumph. He grinned and pointed as snow blew across the elephant's tracks like a frozen sandstorm.

The monastery's iron gate creaked open as we drew near. An elderly monk pushed the heavy metal panel aside and tapped his crooked staff against the ground. He wore open sandals and a patched red cloak that hung off his skinny, bare shoulders. I could only imagine what the ice-wind felt like on his naked, russet-brown skin, but he stood straight and didn't try to brace himself against it.

Before we fled the academy, Mistress Lhamo had warned me that the monks of Chirang had their own brand of magic, a conviction of belief that ran so deep and hot, it coursed through them like liquid fire, making them immune to pain, invincible. She'd urged me not to underestimate them simply because they didn't practice the same magic we did. The old monk seemed to prove what she'd said.

The elephant halted and shook his great head when Pharo attempted to steer him up the slick final slope. The animal's body started to tremble as he took a tentative step forward onto the steep incline. Then he dug his feet into the snow and dropped to his knees.

I drew my cloak tighter around my shoulders. Pharo climbed down first, sinking up to his thighs in white. We tried to maneuver Kalx's limp body to the ground feetfirst—the way Mistress Lhamo had shown us back at the academy. But hours of freezing and stillness had made my fingers clumsy. Kalx's arm slipped through my grasp, and he tumbled into the snow. I bit my lip hard. I wasn't good at caring for Kalx like Pharo was.

I jumped down after him, and my frozen feet hit the ground hard. Numb pain spread through my knees, and I doubled over, rubbing my shins and trying to stomp out the ache. Pharo grimaced, giving me a look of sympathy, and then lifted Kalx. He slung him over his broad shoulders as if my friend weighed nothing. I swallowed down an iron bitterness that could have been blood from my chapped lips or jealousy. I was too cold to care which.

The monk beckoned us toward him. Pharo scrambled forward, but I hesitated, resting my hand on the elephant's side as he shivered in the wind, not moving from his knees. The beast's dark eyes closed.

I wondered if he already knew what would happen to Mistress Lhamo, now that the Myeik were inside the walls of Jakar.

Mistress Lhamo was the oldest of our instructors. She and this once powerful old elephant had been bonded together for over four decades, their souls existing as one. As inhabitors, we all bonded with one animal at the age of eight, and our life force linked to theirs. If the elephant died in the snow, he could spare my teacher the misery of being questioned, auctioned, and sold at the block by the invaders. For my proud, gifted instructor, accustomed to leading and being obeyed, I thought the indignity of slavery would be the worst torture the army could devise.

The elephant let his trunk sag into the snow. He sighed and I couldn't tell if it was with relief or pain.

Pharo grunted under Kalx's weight. "Come on, Tashi."

"We should stay until he passes on. He shouldn't be alone."

"He's not alone. We'd know if he was."

I nodded. The elephant's gentle eyes glittered with intelligence and a kind of grave resignation that was all too human. The cloak I wore suddenly felt too heavy. The wool made my arms itch. I pulled it off and spread it over the animal's wrinkled flank. The creature blinked slowly and reached out for me with his trunk. He smoothed the deft tip across my cheek, and his eyes closed again.

Pharo balanced Kalx by pressing a hand to the small of my friend's back. Then he slipped his other hand into mine. It was comforting, even though it made me feel weaker. We trudged up the hill, onto the ice-covered cobblestones that framed the monastery's entrance. I had to grip Pharo's arm to keep my balance on the slippery ground. He shook his head, smiling when he spoke. "I'm not sure I can support your weight as well as his."

"You'll manage," I croaked, squeezing his arm a little tighter for reassurance. Pharo was built like a bear, solid and muscular with just the right hint of hibernation fat to soften him up. With his striking near-black eyes, dark amber skin, and playful smile, I'd always thought he was gorgeous, but I'd never tell him that. Our friendship was complicated enough.

Raising his arm in a frigid greeting, the monk shuffled toward us through the snow. His body was willowy, nearly skeletal, and his step was light enough that the snow didn't crush under his sandaled feet.

As we drew up alongside him at the gate, he reached out and tugged on a lock of my hair. I winced and cringed back toward Pharo. The monk pressed his lips together, leaning some of his weight onto the staff. "The hair will have to go." He coughed into his sleeve. "You're both going to have to blend in, so if the invaders come here, you'll have camouflage among the rest of our novices. I hope you've studied up on your theology."

I bit my lip, looking at Pharo for help. The day I sealed my own bond with Katala eight years before, I had stopped hiding my identity. Before we bonded, I never had the confidence to talk to anyone about my gender. But linking with Katala gave me the courage to express what I'd always known: that my gender wasn't set, binary. I didn't feel like any of the things people expected of boys or girls fit with me. Some days I felt more masculine and others more feminine. My instructors had been supportive, but it had taken time, pain, and Pharo's hulking glare to convince some of the other students to stop calling me a boy. I didn't want to start over here.

I had always felt like my hair was a visual reminder that I could control. The boys at the academy wore their hair short and neat. The girls had long, untouched locks. My hair was shorn one side of my head, nearly bald, but I grew the other side past my shoulder. It meant that when I looked in the glass each morning, I could turn my head and decide which part of me to see, or look straight ahead and see myself as just me, not forced into anyone's mold. It was a small thing, but it was mine.

I wished Katala were here now. I couldn't let this monk make me hide my identity, not after how I'd struggled to bring it into the light.

Pharo's head jerked up in alarm. "You can't cut their hair—"

The old monk sighed and gave me a look of sympathy. "Your teacher wrote to me about you. But we have to hide you."

"You can't force them." Pharo made a sound in the back of his throat that was almost a growl. He'd always been the first one to my defense, even when we were kids.

"I need…," I began. My breath was shallow, and I felt like my blood was slowing in my veins.

"We have to hide you." The monk glared right through me and the explanation died on my frozen lips. My gaze fell to the snow.

Grunting, the monk poked Kalx's motionless form with the end of his staff. "What's wrong with him? When will he wake?"

Pharo took a step back. "Don't touch him like that."

"He won't," I said, and ice hardened inside me. I wanted to cry, but I couldn't expect Pharo to bear the weight of that too.

I expected the monk to question what I'd said, but instead he just nodded. "*Faelg.*"

The *faelg,* a magical coma, took hold of inhabitors when our bondmates died. No one had ever woken up from it. A week before, one of the Myeik invaders had shot an eagle from the sky. Our legends said that when the bird's heart stopped, Kalx's soul went into mourning—too devastated to care about its host body or emerge again into the light. As inhabitors, our bodies could survive for a while. We didn't pass into the afterlife until our bondmate died too. Pharo believed against the odds that if we took care of Kalx, his soul would remember us and think that maybe his friends were worth living for too. He thought we could break the magical bond. I wished I could be as hopeful.

We all took vows to care for the bodies of others who had entered the coma when we became inhabitors. I'd never understood that vow, since our deaths were inevitable anyway. It seemed almost cruel, to prolong suffering.

"Bring him inside. We will put him in the infirmary." The monk beckoned, and we followed him through the gate into the open courtyard.

A cherry tree stood at the center, in full bloom despite the weather. Pink, red, and white flowers mixed together, alive yet covered in frost. I reached out to pluck a blossom for luck. A jolt of energy pulsed through my fingers, making me drop the soft petal. But before I could touch another, the monk's staff darted out, viper fast and just as vicious, rapping my wrist so hard I could feel a bruise form along the bone.

I cradled my wrist against my chest and swallowed hard.

At the edge of the temple, the monk slipped off his sandals and gestured toward our boots. I removed my own and then knelt to help Pharo. He wobbled under Kalx's weight as he lifted each foot in turn.

The old monk gave another satisfied grunt. As we stepped over the threshold, a young novice came out of the shadows. Like his teacher, he wore his robes hanging off his bare shoulders, but goose bumps covered his exposed flesh. He marched in place to keep warm. The boy motioned to Pharo. "I'll show you to the infirmary."

Grabbing me roughly by the wrist he had smacked, the older monk pulled me along the dim hall while Pharo followed the novice in the other direction. I looked over my shoulder at my friend, silently begging him not to leave me alone, but he'd already turned away.

Inside, the temple had smooth wooden floors swept so clean I couldn't feel even a grain of dirt beneath my bare feet. Statues sitting in a curled lotus position lined the passageway, each overlaid in gold with red smiles carved from ruby. Their cruel emerald eyes followed me as the monk unlocked a plain door at the end of the hall.

"Mistress Lhamo has entrusted us with your safety," he said, setting his staff down against the wall. He shuffled over to a table by the window and picked up a short blade.

Up close, I could see he wasn't as old as I'd thought, but his skin was weathered like well-used leather boots. "She is a friend of mine from many years ago. I feel that I owe it to her, but it's more than that. Thim can't fight the Myeik in open battle and win. We all know that. If we're going to have any chance at all, we have to keep our inhabitors protected."

I nodded, rubbing my cold hands together.

"Sit down," the monk said, pointing to a wooden stool next to the table. He pulled a bucket of half-frozen water from the corner. Then, with unexpected gentleness, he whispered, "I'm sorry."

I backed away from him, pressing my body against the wall. Something in his tone told me I wasn't going to like what he did next. I could almost feel Katala's growl resonating inside me.

"Sit down. Now."

A crawling sensation spread down my back as ghost hackles rose, but my legs betrayed me. With shaking thighs, I sat down on the stool.

The monk poured the water over the blade, watching me instead of the knife as the liquid dripped from the silver edge. His long fingers swept my matted hair back from my eyes. The knife kissed my forehead, and I closed my eyes against the dull scraping that followed.

When I opened them again, a pile of black hair surrounded my feet. Then the monk knelt and swept up the last of my freedom with a dustpan and a little wire brush.

WE SAT apart at dinner, but I had a feeling that Pharo only agreed to that for my sake. He watched the novices devour their bland supper of spiceless rice mixed with goat yogurt, toying with the chopsticks in his bowl. He squirmed in his seat when a pair of older initiates brought out a deck of cards and started to play. Then he inched a fraction closer to them on the bench.

Pharo liked to be popular, liked to engage. He always had.

I ran my hand over my bare scalp and neck. Without my long hair, my head felt too light, almost dizzy. With no hair to hide my face and the new robes falling from my shoulders, I felt exposed, naked instead of holy.

"Where did they make you put Kalx?" I asked, lifting a single grain of the rice to my lips. It tasted of nothing. Even the yogurt lacked sweetness.

"He's in the infirmary. The monk there was giving him a bath when I left. They'll look after him. He might have frostbite in his toes, though." He sighed. "I guess we couldn't help that."

"We shouldn't have taken him from the city. The hospital knew what to do."

Pharo's thick brows knitted together. "He's our best friend, Tashi."

"Was." I focused my gaze on the food again when Pharo's nostrils flared. "No one ever comes back from that."

He looked down at this food, long lashes blinking back pain. Pharo never liked to talk about what happened to us when our bondmates died.

It was something we all were conditioned to understand, even if most of us never fully accepted it. Once you became an inhabitor and said the words of the binding spell, your soul literally fused with another creature's. I could access Katala's memories, feel her emotions, and see what she saw. When she or I died, the one who lived would slip away as Kalx was doing. For me, bonded as I was to a mountain tiger with a projected lifespan of more than thirty years, things didn't seem so bleak. I could live to be forty or maybe older. But Pharo was bonded to a wolf that struggled to chew, with canines rotting in his mouth.

When Pharo went, I would really be alone. I put my chopsticks down and pushed the bowl away.

Pharo gestured to the novices playing cards and smiled in an attempt to lighten my mood. "Hey, we should challenge them. You know you'd win."

"I'm not interested."

"You're great at Tsau! We could try to make friends here—"

"I said I'm not interested," I hissed. "We won't be here long. It's just a halfway house, right? Until the others send word?"

Pharo nodded, but his lips pressed tight. We still didn't know how many of the others from the academy had made it out. With the Myeik soldiers constricting around the city's walls like a great python, not many had managed to escape. With their siege machines, it wouldn't be long until the walls fell too.

A monk so wrinkled and twisted he reminded me of a bonsai tree climbed the dais at the head of the refectory, aided by two novices walking on either side of him. He wore a green robe instead of the red worn by everyone else around us, but it was equally plain. One of the novices helped him settle into an elaborately decorated wooden chair, carved with lotus flowers and set with sapphires. It seemed ironic to me that so much of the temple's design revolved around growing things, when nothing bloomed here other than their treasured cherry tree. The elderly monk lifted his hand for attention, and the murmur in the room went silent. To our right, the novices quickly hid their playing cards under the table.

"We've had a dove this evening," the abbot said. He clutched the arms of the chair. His hands were trembling and covered in spindly veins. "It's over in the city. The central Dzong has been captured."

The novices traded wild glances. One of the bolder young monks raised his hand and blustered, "But, sir, that's… that can't be!"

Pharo sighed, and we exchanged a glance. To the monks, who had only seen it on ceremonial days when the Dzong was covered in gold and flowers, and when abundant free rice wine made everything resplendent, the idea that such a fortress could fall must have seemed impossible. They hadn't seen it at the end like we had.

The academy overlooked the Dzong from a hill. After the catapults had destroyed Jakar's outer walls, the Myeik army set up camp around the Dzong's base, cutting the fortress off from what meager supplies the city had left.

Every morning two officials in green robes had dropped bodies over its great red walls. Every day it seemed like their cheeks grew more hollowed. Kalx used to say that the officials looked like praying mantises in a cage—green, faces drawn together, beady eyes darting skyward, hoping that something edible might fly by.

He meant it as a joke, but nobody had ever laughed when he said it.

"What's happened to everybody? Everybody in the city?" another novice asked, voice shaking. Like us, when the initiates joined the monasteries, they committed for life. We weren't supposed to care about the families we'd had before, but that didn't mean everyone felt that way. In the eyes of the city law, the state was my parent. I could barely even remember what my birth family looked like. My whole life before I joined the academy blurred together in a haze of feelings rather than pictures.

The old monk cleared his throat. "Some of those who survived are quarantined in their houses. Mostly the children and those too sick to work."

"And the others? The adults who lived?"

"They are being auctioned... sold."

I thought of the elephant, lying down to die outside the monastery. I felt a wash of nostalgia and affection. He'd spared Mistress Lhamo the indignity of standing on an auctioneer's block after they broke her spirit in the torture chambers. As an inhabitor, she would have been a prize to a wealthy Myeik, despite her age. As far as we'd seen, they didn't really know how our powers worked, but they knew we had them, and that was enough to make us valuable.

If it came to it, would Katala sacrifice herself to save me from going through life like that? Suddenly I was overwhelmed with the need to check on her. A knot of guilt twisted in my stomach. Here I was, wondering if she'd save me from torture, and I hadn't even examined her for wounds since she'd defended me from the Myeik archers. I'd been more concerned with reaching the monastery and sinking into a hot bath. What if she was injured? Some bondmate I was.

A bloom of silver sparks shot up around me. The image of a wandering farm cow flashed through my mind. My heart began to beat faster in anticipation. Katala abruptly closed our connection. She was busy, and I'd slowed her down on the hunt. The silver particles dropped like hailstones onto the table.

Strong fingers closed around my bicep. From nowhere, the monk who had shaved my head pulled me off the bench. My weight fell backward as he jerked me roughly to my feet. Pharo quickly swept up all the drops of metal with his hand, closing his fist around the fresh silver. Then the monk dragged me from the room before anyone had the chance to speak.

Outside the refectory, he slapped my face. "What were you thinking? I say you need to blend in, so you use your magic?"

The sting was intense and sharp. I yelped. "What? I needed to see how she was!"

"You can't do that here! I know about you, and the abbot knows. That's it. The novices think you are transfers from a monastery in the south that burned down. If the Myeik soldiers come here, how long do you think your secret will last? The initiates gossip worse than grandmothers in a knitting circle!"

"It's too late now anyway. They all saw."

"They were focused on the abbot, and they're upset. They won't realize what they saw. None of them have ever seen an inhabitor connect." The monk shook his head, cursing. "Mistress Lhamo told me to watch out for you in particular. You were special to her, to all the instructors. 'Hide them, Ugyen,' she wrote, 'we'll need them.' Don't make me break a promise."

I hung my head as my other cheek started to burn as well. That letter might have been the last one my teacher ever wrote. Keeping me safe had been her dying wish. "I didn't think."

"Think next time. You might not get another chance to make a mistake." Ugyen tilted my chin up to look at him. "In the meantime, do that in private. Only when you and Pharo are alone."

I'd spent the last seven years learning to make the connection flow between us as naturally as water. Now he wanted me to wall it all up. I wondered how I could make Katala understand. She didn't accept new rules without an explanation, and although our bond had increased her understanding, she only knew a few dozen human words. Or at least she pretended that was all she understood.

"I'll try."

"Do better than try. We will need your abilities in this war. But until they're called on, you need to hide them. Or you'll die before you ever get the chance to be useful."

I looked toward the door, trying to escape his grip. "I will."

His fingers tightened on my chin. His nails dug into my skin. "Good. You inhabitors are our ears, and you spread power through our soil. We need at least some of you to stay alive if we have any chance of rebuilding this mess of a country after the invaders go. In the meantime, I'm going to keep you so busy with chores you won't even have time to sleep, much less do that again. Your bones will ache with tiredness, and connecting will be the last thing on your mind. You might not even be able to do it."

He released me. My hand flew to my cheek, and I pressed my cold palm against the burn.

When I first joined the academy, everyone always said that our abilities were a blessing. Our lives were short, but we lived two at once, and we experienced the world with an intensity most humans could never imagine. Beyond that, for as long as we were alive, people revered us. Even when the Myeik laid siege to the capitol, we were the only ones who could escape the living hell inside the walls. Even if our bodies were trapped in the city, our minds could take us wherever we wanted.

Today was the first day I'd ever truly felt trapped.

CHAPTER 2

THE DAY I became an inhabitor, Mistress Lhamo had carried me into the forest outside the capitol and left me there. I was eight and small, so small that the robes the academy gave me swathed my body and made me look like a slug as I trailed fabric behind. She set me down on a tree stump and kissed my hair. Then she had wandered back through the trees to the city without a second glance. I guessed, then, I had been expendable to her. If I didn't work out, then Jakar had plenty more poor children and orphans to choose from.

I held a ragged stuffed owl against my chest as I shivered and prayed, repeating the words of the spell I'd been taught. Master Amo thought I might attract a doe or a hare. Something agile, he said, but shy and timid. Something to match me so I wouldn't feel conflicted within myself. I just hoped nothing would eat me and that Mistress Lhamo would return soon.

Sunlight dwindled, and the forest got darker and colder. I paced around the stump. The terror of being eaten had ebbed, replaced by the more insidious fear that I wouldn't be chosen at all, that the rest of my friends would go on to be inhabitors and I would become an outcast—a failure with nowhere to go and doomed to a life of begging on the street corners.

I threw the owl on the ground. It had been a present from Master Amo when he selected me two years before. If they were going to reject me now, then I didn't want the stuffed bird anymore either.

The wind carried a pungent scent into my nostrils. It was sweet yet musky, tinged with something sour. I breathed more deeply and looked around for the source. At the edge of the forest clearing, a deer carcass lay stretched out and mutilated. Her throat had been torn out, and dark brown blood was splashed over her tan hide. Even in death, the doe had a calm, gentle look in her unblinking eyes. I had bitten my lip and struggled not to cry. There was my doe, just like Master Amo had said.

A growl made me turn. A large, lean cat with rose-gold and white fur lowered its belly to the earth. Its yellow eyes bored into me, and its tail flickered back and forth. I sucked in a breath. I'd seen a tiger up close before, rubbing its cheeks against Master Lin's thigh before it turned and snarled at an apprentice who drew too close. But that tiger had been orange and black, normal. This creature looked like something out of a temple painting, as though her fur had been expertly flecked with tiny pieces of gold leaf by a monk's skilled hand.

The animal's haunches had tensed. Her legs had gathered to pounce. But instead of terror, I felt calm. She tackled me, pushing me down with an enormous paw. Her claws were sheathed, and the pad of her foot rested over my heart. My breath stopped as I understood late what it all meant. The tiger rolled me onto my back like a cub, licking my chin with her barbed tongue. My arms, still chubby with baby fat, curled around her neck.

When her weight settled over me, I felt the acceptance in the silky embrace of her fur. And for the first time since I left my real family, I felt something like love. But her message was clear: I would never control her. From that moment, when our souls connected and I became an inhabitor, I knew I was the vulnerable one and she would forever be protecting me.

MY EYES ran, skin peeled from my fingers, and my knees felt as though I knelt on kernels of rice. Beside me, Pharo swiped at his nose with his wrist. His brown hands were also chafed from the harsh soap we worked into the floors. I dipped my rag into the bucket of water. The icy liquid burned almost as much as the soap. Manual labor had never been part of our program at the academy. Our skins were soft, without the dense calluses I'd seen on some of the novices' palms. At least Pharo had played sports. I winced and slipped my fingers under my armpits to warm them.

"This is your fault," Pharo grumbled. He tossed his rag into the pail and leaned back against the wall. Sweat formed a dew-like film on his bald head, now shaved as mine was. It looked good on him. "If you hadn't opened your connection at dinner yesterday, Ugyen wouldn't think we were such a risk."

"I didn't know," I snapped. He'd been repeating that all afternoon. "Can you just drop it? I said I was sorry."

Pharo blew into his palms. "They haven't even fed us since breakfast. The sun's going down. And what's with this no meat thing they do here?"

"It's probably hard to raise lots of animals here," I said. Humans were barred from hunting in Thim. A wild pig snared by a farmer could be linked to an inhabitor, and then its slaughter counted as murder. Other animals, even those not tied to an inhabitor, could tell the difference. But as humans, our instincts were dull. We only ate the beasts we raised.

"What else do they have to do?" Pharo gestured at the spotlessly clean hall around us. "Besides polish this place up when it doesn't need it."

"We should ask Katala and Faern to migrate closer... then they could hunt for us." Katala was a nomad at heart, never settling, always looking for a new adventure. She would relish the chance to explore the mountains, far away from the noise and chaos of the city.

"What are you thinking? These monks would be furious if they caught us sneaking into the woods."

"They haven't checked on us all day." I threw my own rag into the bucket and moved into the single line of sun creeping through the temple window. I stretched, warming myself like a cat.

When Pharo's scowl deepened, I winked. He was used to me being the cautious one, but hunger gave me courage. Pharo crossed his arms over his broad chest. "I know that look, Tashi. And whenever you start stretching and yawning and acting like that tiger, I get worried.

You're usually not reckless. When that happens, I know Katala's influencing you."

I grinned at him. Arguing with him like this felt normal, like something we used to do between lessons on the common green. I allowed myself to relax. "Scoot over by the door and keep watch."

"No way!"

"There's nobody else here." I gritted my teeth. Pharo's stomach rumbled, and he squirmed. "Meat. Think about meat. Rabbit... maybe a mountain goat."

I knew all of this was a risk, but my cheek was still sore where Ugyen had slapped me, and I wouldn't go hungry as well. Not when I was linked to a ruthless hunter with claws like dinner knives. I wasn't sure how we would cook the meat, but that was a problem for later.

"Fine." Pharo inched closer to the entrance to the temple hall. "But a minute only. If you're with Kat too long, I'll slap you until you come back."

I shrugged. "I won't feel it. Not much, anyway."

Pharo raised his eyebrow. "You will when your thoughts come back to this body. You'll wake up bruised."

I curled my aching legs under my body and breathed deeply. In some things, we shared the customs of the monks. All of us learned to meditate as soon as we entered the academy. While I could forge a connection anywhere, it was deeper, fuller when the mind was empty and the body still. I stole a final glance toward the door before my eyes rolled back.

I CROUCHED on a ledge, overlooking that familiar steep hill and the enclosed monastery below. The world spun around me as my thoughts settled in the new body. Snowflakes melted on my fur and stuck in my whiskers. A shudder of excitement went through our shared body as I realized Katala had already followed me into the mountains. She had a way of always anticipating what I would need her to do. I scanned the rocks below, looking for the best way to wind my way to the ground. But when I tried to take a step, my body remained motionless, kept in position by the other consciousness governing it.

My head turned, but my paws dug into the snow. I looked down and squinted at the narrow path leading up to the monastery. The elephant's body lay at the base of the hill. A pool of frozen blood and entrails lay around it, seeping from a jagged opening in the creature's belly. I yawned and suddenly became aware of the weight of a large meal making my stomach hang low enough to brush the snow. Even though Katala had known the elephant—had allowed him to stroke her fur with the tip of his gentle trunk—tigers felt no loyalty to the dead.

Beyond the elephant's half-eaten carcass, a yellow flag billowed. A moment later, I smelled the sweetgrass musk of horses carried through on the wind. I felt my muscles tense, and without warning, my body leaped from the outcrop onto a lower ledge and pressed itself against the mountain. For a moment after the unexpected movement, vertigo made all the yellow objects below blur together. Then I made out men and women on horses riding up the mountain, each wearing the mustard yellow army cloak of the Myeik elite force. An endless column of them filed in pairs through the pass. Their clothing stuck to their sweat-covered bodies. Their skin smelled of garlic, metal, and cow meat.

At the head of the column, a man with a plumed headdress rode the biggest horse I'd ever seen. The creature's fur was red and strewn with white hairs. Long, wispy feathers framed hooves bigger than dinner bowls. The horse tried to shy away from the elephant's mutilated body, but the commander kicked it roughly on. The animal's hooves screeched as metal shoes scraped ice.

My lips parted. Katala's roar echoed through me before a jolt of pain sent my thoughts fleeing back to my seated human body.

PHARO PUNCHED my shoulder and then aimed another blow to my gut. I coughed, lurching forward and nearly vomiting on our newly polished floor. Drops of metal hit the ground around us. Pharo wiped them up with his rag and tossed them into the water bucket. It seemed wasteful to throw away pure silver, but I didn't want Ugyen to see.

When we got older and developed more control, nothing could break our concentration or our bonds. For inhabitors as skilled as Mistress Lhamo, her body could endure torture, burning, and she would never feel it. But my skills weren't quite so honed yet, and Pharo knew that.

"You took your sweet time," he said, and I noticed his chest was heaving. "I was trying everything to wake you up. Something's going on outside. A bunch of the monks came running past while you were off. But they didn't stop to look at us."

A handful of novices tiptoed into the hall on bare feet, toes purple with cold. They whispered together and clustered by the window to peer outside. They ignored our presence, stepping around us like we were nothing more than statues. Perhaps this was part of the punishment.

"Get back to what you were doing, all of you." Ugyen strode into the hall. He clapped his hands, then parted the novices with his staff like a herd of goats. "The senior monks will handle this and tell you what to do."

"Master Ugyen," I said, forcing myself to my feet. I tried not to cower at the sneer on his face. "I saw—"

"Don't tell me what you saw. Duck your heads. Don't stare. Don't provoke." He bent down to swipe a finger over an unclean patch of floor. "When they come in, you are no one—a disobedient temple servant, that is all. Remember it. Scrub."

Striding to the door, Ugyen wrenched it open and stepped outside. As the novices craned around him to listen, he pulled it tightly closed. The younger monks dispersed. They spoke to one another in hushed, disappointed whispers and funneled toward the refectory.

I started to get up, to follow them to a needed meal. I was in a daze from what I'd seen, and I wanted to hide. It couldn't be possible that we'd hidden in the most remote place Mistress Lhamo could imagine, only to have the invaders catch up with us in the space of a day.

"He said to scrub." Pharo gripped my arm and yanked me back to the floor. His midnight eyes bored into mine. "What did you see? Tell me."

"They're here," I whispered. "The army."

"What?" Pharo hissed. He scooted closer to me across the damp floor. "How is it possible?"

I shook my head, glancing toward the refectory again. "We should go."

"No." His hold on my wrist tightened. "We're trained to spy. We need to stay. We need to see what they're after."

"What if they're after us?" I hissed.

The temple door creaked, and the brass handle turned. I looked at Pharo and tried to plead telepathically with him to let me go while there was still time to run. But he held fast, eyes narrowing into slits as he waited for the enemy.

CHAPTER 3

I KEPT my eyes lowered as the door to the hall swung open. Nervous energy danced through me. I wasn't sure what to expect. Part of me imagined a legion storming through the monastery and snatching us up like prized jewels to take back to the capitol in chains.

Instead, only two pairs of feet marched toward the place where Pharo and I sat. One set belonged to Ugyen. His feet were bare, murky brown with a gnarled mole on one big toe. He padded across the wood floors as silently as a rat slinking away, trying to avoid the eye of its predator. The stranger wore thick boots with steel caps. Fine serrated blades stuck out from the metal toe. I wondered whether they were for show, or if this man was the type to use them as a weapon, kicking someone to death with the kind of savagery we had learned that only the Myeik army possessed. The newcomer left muddy footprints with every arrogant stride. A line of brown water trickled across the glossy surface of our polished floor and pooled by Pharo's knee.

"You will condense your people into one building so that we can set up our troops and hospital in the other," the man said. He stopped to look down at us. *Don't look up*, I willed myself. *Don't look into his eyes. Be invisible.*

The door swung open again, and a flurry of servants burst in with the cold wind. They scuttled to the commander's side and flanked him like a group of ducklings in their yellow army cloaks.

The commander pointed to me and then turned to Ugyen. "I thought I told you to move all the novices into the refectory so I could speak to them after I carried out my inspection."

"All the novices are there, Commander," Ugyen said, clearly thinking fast. He wrung his hands once and then picked at a loose string on his robes to keep his fingers from betraying his nerves. The way he simpered after the enemy commander sickened me. I wondered if he or the abbot had put up any resistance at all, or just allowed these city-rapers to stroll through the gates. They hadn't allowed us to hear their discussions outside. "These are just servants. They are not at rest with the others as they disobeyed the abbot."

Suddenly, a riding crop darted out. I flinched, but the commander lifted my chin with the soft leather and forced me to look at him. I swallowed down terror. His face was young, beardless. I noticed the smoothness of it—he didn't look old enough to have been in battle at all, much less risen to the rank of commander. He had blue-green eyes and light, freckled skin. He studied me in turn and then crouched down for a closer look. His fingers replaced the crop under my chin, and he turned my face to the side. I closed my eyes and tried to distance myself from the humiliation of his inspection.

When he took hold of my wrist, I nearly cried out from the pain. Yellow burns covered my raw palms.

"What's wrong with your hands? Do you have a sickness?" He didn't wait for an answer, turning to Ugyen instead. "What is wrong with him? You assured us this place was clear of disease and would be appropriate for our purposes."

I cleared my throat, annoyance at being talked around giving me a voice. "No... Commander... sir... it's from this soap that we used on the floor."

Ugyen flushed, and I was glad looking at my blisters made him ashamed.

Shoulders relaxing, the commander turned my hand over. His grip gentled. "He'll do."

"They," Pharo piped up from the floor beside me. I could have kissed him but Ugyen cast us a cutting glare.

"Excuse me?" the commander demanded.

"Tashi isn't a boy."

The commander's lips twitched. "I thought you Thim were still centuries behind with your ideas about sexuality and gender. Maybe our influence here is doing more good than you like to admit."

I was relieved that Pharo had spoken up for me, but I hated this arrogant boy-commander's smirk and his condescension. As if the Myeik had anything to teach us beyond warfare. My own people had learned to accept me long before his soldiers set foot on our land.

A lean scribe behind him looked me over and made a note on the ledger he held against his chest.

Ugyen shifted from foot to foot. "They'll do for what?"

"I'll need a servant to wait on me. Mine is dead. And I'll be using the abbot's chambers."

The casual way he spoke of his servant's death made my skin crawl. There was no emotion in his voice, and his strange eyes gave away nothing. Nothing indicated that he'd cared for that man at all. I wondered how quickly he would dispose of me. How had the other man died?

"They are a dirty urchin. Surely, if you are looking for a valet, someone else might be more suitable—"

The commander lifted a gloved hand. "That one. And I never said a valet."

I shivered and moved closer to Pharo's bulk. But despite his size and strength, there was nothing he could do for me now. I noticed the angry, set line of his jaw. He knew it as well as I did.

"Of course." Ugyen bowed his head, and I saw defeat in the slump of his back. By trying to keep us invisible and out of sight, he had drawn the commander's attention right to us. "Perhaps we could speak on the matter of the abbot? He's an old man. He can't stay in the catacombs for long…."

The commander ignored him, leaned over to his steward, and pointed to me. "They will need to be washed. Have them cleaned and put in the abbot's old chambers for me."

His words made the hairs on my arms stand up. He spoke of me like I was an object, something for him to play with. Pharo lifted his gaze and stared openly. Why did I need to be washed? And why did he want me in his rooms? During the invasion, at night when they thought all of us were asleep, some of the instructors used to whisper about the Myeik and their strange customs.

I tried to ask, "What will you do to me?" but the bitter words stuck to my tongue.

STILL SHIVERING from the icy bath two of the Myeik stewards had given me, I opened the heavy oak door to the abbot's old suite and stepped inside. Although I'd never been in his rooms before, it was obvious that someone had hastily rearranged the chamber. Bronze statues of the gods faced the walls, isolated in a small corner. Tapestries in rich blues and greens, depicting the creation of Jakar, lay strewn across the floor like cheap carpets. The drawers in the wardrobe and side table had been thrown open and emptied. Thick furs from bears and wolves, which no monk could touch without offending the gods, adorned the mahogany bed.

I pressed my body up against the wall, trying to step around the tapestries. In the time before—the time I wasn't supposed to think about now that I was an inhabitor—my mother used to spin the lotus fibers for cloths like these.

At the far side of the room, I sank into a cushioned bench. Rippled glass filled the window, making the outside world look like a painted canvas covered by raindrops. I turned the chair to face the door and backed it against the far wall. Having learned from Katala's hunts, I knew better than to leave too many sides of myself exposed to a predator.

In the room's silence, I could almost hear my heart in my chest. This was the first time I'd been alone since Pharo and I fled from the academy. Normally I would have welcomed the solitude. Instead I chewed the white tips of my nails as the silence ate away at me.

I pressed my hand to my head as a searing pain pulsed behind my eyes: Katala wanting to push into the bond, to connect. The longer I ignored her, the more the pain would intensify. I wanted nothing more than to reach out for her. When I was in Katala's body, I felt powerful. As a tiger, I was enveloped by fur, equipped with claws and senses so acute I could smell the tepid sulfur of another's fear. In my own form, I felt weak and exposed.

I looked toward the door, watching the crack underneath for movement. By the time it opened, I'd bitten my nails almost down to the beds. The commander stepped through, and I took a breath to steady my nerves. I was an inhabitor—a trained spy and shifter. What was all our education for, if not to prepare us for this? I would survive in order to watch. Unbidden, my eyes started to sting as the commander stripped off his military coat and threw it on the bed. Tremors spread through my body. I'd never thought *this* was something I'd have to survive.

"What's your name?" he asked. Although he got all the words right, his tongue slurred the phrase together. His accent was strong.

"Tashi."

He repeated it. Suddenly I couldn't even look at him. Listening to him saying my name made it all the more real.

"You may wonder why I would want a foreign servant rather than simply choose a new one from among those brought by my men."

I closed my eyes as a bitter taste filled my mouth.

"Do you speak my language? Read it?"

I could. Compared with the intricate, precise system of symbols and columns we used in Thim, the Myeik system of letters was simple to learn and read. With its poetic flow and soft vowels, Myeik had always been one of my favorite languages to study before the invasion. But a good spy never revealed it to be so. Even through the haze of fear, I heard Mistress Lhamo's instructions ring in my ears. I shook my head.

"Good. Our army is full of people who want to get ahead and get promotions. In the military, all the officers employ servants who can't speak our tongue. It means that anything I say in private stays that way." He leaned down and began unfastening his boots. "I'll have a pallet brought in for you."

A pallet. A word that should have made me feel relief since at least I wouldn't be expected to sleep next to this monster when he finished with me. But something about the idea of being tossed on the floor like a dog after he used me made everything worse.

Cringing, I looked up. His strange eyes were hawkish, narrowed with confusion. Then he sighed. "I know what you think. You're not here for that. Everyone in Jakar seems to think the worst of us because of what some unruly soldiers have done in the city. You are here to fetch things. Take messages. Clean. Pour drinks. When we move on, I will probably leave you behind if that's what you still want. Though from how I've seen you are treated here, you might decide it is better to move on with us."

Air flooded through my lungs.

"I'm Xian." The commander lifted his foot and began to rub the sole. "You can call me that in private. It'd be nice to hear someone my age say it again. You look about my age. What are you—sixteen? Seventeen?"

Again I took in the sight of him, the smooth chin and youthfully slender build. Relief made me stupid, and the words escaped before I could stop them. I blurted, "You're too young to be leading an army."

He laughed, flexing his toes. "It's only one unit I lead, and we're left to babysit the wounded most of the time. Command comes with family status in Myeik. I was born knowing how to lead."

"That doesn't sound efficient."

He raised an eyebrow. "It's not. But still, we're winning."

I closed my mouth on another response. Back at the academy, Master Amo had often scoffed at the Myeik idea of victory. *What do they win,* he had asked, mouth full of red tobacco leaves, *if they burn everything worth taking?* I didn't dare share that with Xian.

Clearing his throat, he said, "It's freezing up here. Is that all they give you to wear?"

I drew the red cloak tighter to my chest, hoping he couldn't see the bumps on my skin or the network of blue veins. Novices and temple servants joined the monastery at seven. Real monks would be used to the temperature in the mountains by now, or so I guessed. "I barely feel the cold anymore," I murmured.

"Well, it makes me cold just looking at you. You haven't taken the vows anyway, so why do you have to dress like that? I'll have one of the men bring you something heavier." He lay back on the bed, closing his eyes.

I allowed myself to relax into the chair. A stiff pain crept up my spine from the hours spent scrubbing the floor. Xian was the enemy, but so far, Ugyen had treated me worse. Xian didn't know what I was, had no suspicions. Maybe this was the best way for me to hide: right under the enemy's nose, serving their wine. If a regiment commander vouched for me, who would question me?

Sitting up again, Xian sighed and stuffed his feet back into his boots. He regarded me for a second. There were questions in his gaze, but one blink of his long eyelashes swept them away. "I need to inspect the hospital ward. Take me there before I get too comfortable and can't make myself get up."

I nodded and got shakily to my feet. That morning I had seen Pharo emerge from the ward after he'd gone to check on Kalx, but I'd never been inside. I prayed that I could find it again in the labyrinth of halls, prayer rooms, and enclosed gardens. Because if I couldn't, what would he think? And what would he do?

He followed me down the hallway, stopping now and then to run a finger over one of the statues or inspect a tapestry. His expression didn't appreciate, it appraised. I wondered when the things—and people—in this monastery, like everything else in Jakar, would go to the auction block. I heard him talking about something, asking questions maybe, but his words flowed past me like wind as I struggled to piece together the incomplete map in my head.

As we turned the corner down an empty corridor, I saw a flash of white ahead and breathed a sigh of relief. The hospital was as Pharo had described it, with plain white walls and an open window looking toward the cherry tree at the center of the courtyard—the monks believed that emptiness facilitated healing.

I tried not to stare at Kalx as we entered the ward. He looked so fragile. The bones in his chest showed under flesh that drooped from starvation. I couldn't reconcile this person with my plump, energetic friend.

A young initiate lay on the cot next to him, crying softly as an older monk bandaged a cut on his thigh. The boy practically choked on his tears at the sight of Xian. The old monk's fingers stopped winding the strips of fabric around the wound and trembled as they hovered in the air.

Xian gestured to Kalx. "What happened to him?"

The older monk didn't speak, and the small novice just continued to cry.

When the incident had first happened, I'd battled tears every time I looked at Kalx's body. Even now, I had to bite my lip to keep the pain inside me from spilling out. I knew we couldn't fight the magic that cursed him, but sometimes I wished for a sliver of Pharo's hope.

Xian walked around the cot and rested his pale hand on Kalx's chest. I watched his face as he monitored the steadiness of my friend's breath and took in the glassy look in Kalx's open eyes. A sponge rested next to him on the bed. Someone had to wet Kalx's lips and coax food down his throat every day to keep him alive.

"When will he wake?" Xian asked, but again, none of us answered him.

A knock came on the wall outside the ward's open door. Pharo walked in, eyes lowered, with a bowl of rice pudding cupped in his huge palm. I could smell the cream from where I sat, and my stomach complained. He sat down on the edge of the cot. Then he lifted Kalx from under the arms and manipulated his body into a sitting position.

"When will he wake?" Xian demanded, a rough edge to his voice this time. He looked directly at Pharo.

"Never," my friend whispered. He blew on a spoonful of the mixture and lifted it to Kalx's dry lips.

Xian looked to me. "Is that true?"

I nodded, blinking slowly to force back a sudden tsunami of emotion and memories.

Xian sat down on the cot beside Pharo. Glancing behind him to the elderly monk, he pointed to the boy with the injured leg and ordered, "Both of you, take the boy out."

"Sir?" The monk's reedy voice quivered.

"Out," Xian growled, pointing to the open door.

The old man struggled to his feet, balancing on a staff.

Xian's fingers wrapped around the throwing dagger at his belt. Fear churned inside my empty belly. How did someone become so used to giving orders at such a young age? When Pharo hesitated, Xian's eyes burned into him. When he spoke again, the commander's voice was as quiet as a snake's hiss. "Take him outside. Now."

Pharo got up and went to the child, hoisting him from the bed. He looked to me with worry in his golden eyes. He tried to mouth something, but I couldn't catch his question.

Xian scooted closer to Kalx on the cot. He rested his hand on my friend's forehead and said something in Myeik, but he spoke too quietly for me to hear the words. He closed Kalx's eyelids and then fished in his purse for something.

He removed two coins from his purse and laid them on Kalx's eyelids. I wondered if this was some kind of prayer. Although we had studied their military habits, their language, and some of their customs, I knew little of the Myeik religion. No one really did. They kept no statues and built no temples. There was nothing tangible for our scholars to examine, and they never sent ambassadors here who could explain.

In a flash of movement so quick I had no chance to stop him, Xian pulled his dagger from his belt and drew the blade across Kalx's throat. My friend began to choke, a gurgling noise emitting from deep inside him. His body convulsed as the blood flowed down his windpipe… drowning him. More blood spurted from the wound, soaking into the wool blankets like red ink into a rice-paper sheet. The color drained from his cheeks.

I rushed through the open door and into the courtyard. I ran as far as the base of the cherry tree before my knees gave way. I sank to the ground and vomited at the tree's roots. Xian watched me silently from the open window, his lips pressed together.

CHAPTER 4

HOURS LATER, I listened while the murderer snored. My cheeks were stiff with dry, salty tears. As promised, one of his lieutenants had delivered a pallet, a pair of breeches, and a fur cloak finer and softer than anything I'd ever worn. It was odd that no guard watched Xian while he slept. But then again, I supposed that a boy-commander assigned to occupying a remote monastery couldn't really be all that important to the operations of the army. And I already knew how they must see me. I was no threat, a temple servant, pledged to the gods, a defenseless monk, too much a pacifist even to eat meat. I drew the mink fur tighter, imagining Katala slept curled around me.

He'd tossed at first, but now Xian's breath was quiet and steady. A familiar pain pulsed behind my eyes, sharp and insistent. Katala hated being ignored and would push harder and harder until I answered her. She could sense my stillness and my grief.

I glanced around the room and then rose to my feet. The abbot had his own privy, separated from the rest of the suite by a thin rice-paper door. A board creaked under my feet as I moved toward it, but Xian didn't stir. He grasped a pillow under one arm, callused feet poking out from under the thick wool blanket. If I hadn't just seen him slit Kalx's throat in cold blood, I could almost believe that he was peaceful. I hadn't dared to ask him about it.

I stepped into the privy and closed the door behind me. Through the thin screen, I knew Xian would be able to see my outline but not the vacant look in my eyes or the tears of metal forming in the air. I sat on the privy, wrinkling my nose in disgust. No one had emptied the abbot's privy in a few days, and the stench hovered.

Relaxing my back and leaning against the wall, I reached for Katala. Her response was swift, impatient. As soon as my thoughts settled in her body, she moved, an excitement in her step as we trotted through the snow. There was something she'd been waiting all day to show me.

We darted behind a rock and into Katala's temporary den. She never stayed in one place long enough to carve out a territory or find a mate. Her nomadic spirit matched her role as an inhabitor's bondmate, although I sometimes felt sorry that she would never experience a full tiger's life with a territory or cubs of her own. Then again, maybe she pitied me in the same way.

Crawling forward on her belly, Katala took us deep into the cave she'd claimed. Icy stalactites lined the mouth, and the floor froze the pads of her paws. The cave was midnight black, and if I had been in my own body, I never would have been able to make out the flash of metal at the back of the den. I squinted toward it, sniffing the air. Despite the warmth of Katala's thick fur, I shivered. The smell was unmistakable: blood.

Our teeth sank into half-frozen flesh, cutting through muscle and fat, meeting bone. Strings of the decaying meat lodged themselves between our canines. I felt queasy and swallowed down a bitter dread. The taste was a mixture of salt and something sour. I tried to unlock our shared jaws and to stop Katala from dragging into sight what I knew was coming....

A man. Determinedly, Katala pulled her prize into the middle of the cave floor. I studied him through the lens of her proud gaze, feeling disconnected from her even though I still inhabited her body. She had torn off most of his armor, but links of chain mail were frozen to the clotted blood forming red ice crystals on his skin. His head lolled to one side, nearly severed from his neck by the deep wound that gaped from his throat.

I searched her memories as Katala lay down next to her prey, body vibrating with happy rumbles. Tigers didn't purr like housecats, but Katala made a noise between a growl and a hum when things pleased her. Through our bank of shared thoughts, I watched her creep along the forest line as she tracked a lone sentry. The vision was so real, I could nearly feel the crunch of frosted leaves beneath my paws, hear the man's muffled scream, and sense the last pulse of his wildly thumping heart.

Panic clawed at me. How long before the Myeik noticed he was missing? With his body so deep down in the earth, guarded by a man-eating golden tiger, I doubted that anyone would find the corpse. But if Katala and I were one soul, was I a murderer now in the eyes of the gods? Or did it count as a battle killing, since this man was an enemy? We'd killed before, together, in the heat of battle. I hadn't thought anything of it then. Not when it was kill or be killed. But this man hadn't even had the time to unsheathe his blade.

Mistress Lhamo would have known the answers.

Katala growled. She'd expected joy from me—and praise.

I remembered the elephant, lying down in the snow to die with such dignified resignation. He'd saved his friend of decades from torture at the hands of the same army that now occupied this quiet monastery in the mountains. I was an inhabitor, a trained spy, and a soldier. I could fight them, and it would be just no matter what the field of battle looked like. But just the thought of initiating an attack on someone who was unprepared, just going about their day, made my insides churn again. That elephant had more courage than I ever would.

I broke the connection. The paper screen blocking Xian and the room from view remained fixed in place. I scooped up the metal stones and threw them down the abbot's privy, holding my nose. Inhabitors never struggled for money or coin. Back at the academy, we kept them and used the silver we produced to trade at the market. We were taught that it was the gods' payment for our sacrifice. But here I couldn't risk collecting my pound of ethereal coin. A rush of dizziness hit me as I struggled to my feet. Bracing myself against the wall, I took a deep breath and slowly opened the door.

Xian still lay in the same position. A small smile played at the corner of his lips, and his foot twitched.

I crawled onto the pallet, trying in vain to fluff up the flat military-issue pillow. I'd trained for this, in theory, but Jakar hadn't been at war in three hundred years. We'd had a golden age of peace, where inhabitors trained but never fought. What did we really know about war or spying or rebellion anymore?

For the last eight years of my life, I'd studied tactics, practiced meditation, and learned to make detailed reports. Movement came naturally to me in the bodies of two species, and I could speak six languages. But when the invaders knocked down the city walls, all our training proved useless in the face of weapons no one in Jakar had ever imagined.

Yet here I was, sleeping like some sort of pet at the foot of the enemy's bed.

I pulled the blanket up to my chin and continued to watch Xian as he slept. Even in sleep, his fingers curled loosely around a dagger. Moonlight caught the hilt, and it glittered, half-hidden by his pillow.

I stuffed the hem of the wool blanket into my mouth to stifle a cry. Why did Katala have to be so aggressive, so suited to her role? Not for the first time, I wished she had chosen someone else. I thought back to the deer she'd killed in the clearing on the day of our meeting, with its gentle eyes. Surely the gods had been joking when they sent a golden tiger to me. Fate had positioned me perfectly, but I wasn't brave enough for this.

A POUNDING on the door woke me some time later. I sat up, confused by the sunspots dancing in my vision and a lingering headache. At the academy, the bells rang to wake us every morning. We lived our lives in time to those bells: morning, noon, meals, meditation, and classes—even our illusory "free time" was governed by a brass gong on the side of a hill. My headache pulsed as if an independent heart beat behind my temple, but Xian's covers lay strewn across the floor. I could see his outline through the paper screen. Katala would have to wait.

My muscles screamed as I climbed to my feet. Academy beds were soft, padded with lamb's wool and covered in goat pelts. The pallet was barely an inch thick. Someone had lit the fire in the grate, and now the room was oppressively hot. I didn't think I'd recovered yet from Ugyen's hard enforced labor. It had been only one day, but my body was soft, and at the academy I never exercised unless required. Inhabitors could engage in combat training if they chose, but since I was bonded with a tiger, I never bothered. It wasn't like I'd ever be any good in a physical fight compared to her. Massaging my lower back, I stumbled to the door and wrenched it open. A blast of cold air froze the sweat as it dripped down my forehead.

Dressed in yellow and silver livery, a military steward balanced a steaming tray. His lip was curled back, and his nose wrinkled as the wind carried the smell of meat toward me. Sneering, he thrust the tray into my hands. "Here, take this and serve it to the commander. Make yourself useful."

Dumplings wrapped in gooey pastry, and rice noodles as fine as strands of hair… the scents of orange and plum sauces whispered into my nostrils. Saliva pooled in my mouth.

"It's for the commander," the steward said. He pinched my ear viciously between his nails. "If he deigns to feed you, that's his decision. But you'd best not start eating what isn't yours. I expect the monks will keep something for you somewhere."

Tears of pain tingled in my eyes. I tried to blink them away, but a drop of water hooked onto my eyelash and wriggled down my cheek.

The steward rolled his eyes and then spat on the ground at my feet. "Weak. All of you in this country, so very, very weak. In Myeik, we're born with steel in our bones."

I had to bite my tongue to hold back a retort. We had culture, and science, and Dzongs that were the envy of the world, a little voice inside me protested, but a louder doubt drowned it out. The Myeik had science too; they'd proved it with the battle machines they rolled to our gates. Weak. A little pinch and I was already crying like an infant in front of the enemy—there was no way I was going to survive this.

He pushed the door open for me with a brittle laugh. "Run along, little one."

I backed away from him into the chambers. I looked at my feet as more tears spilled down. My back collided with something warm and solid. An overripe dragon fruit rolled onto the floor. I turned around slowly. Then my cheeks went hot because I knew Xian could see the tears on my face. I couldn't be a spy. I wasn't even capable of being a room servant, much less gathering secrets. Xian was sure to get rid of me and pick someone more suitable like Ugyen said.

"Hey, did he hurt you?" Xian tilted my chin up to examine my face, as he'd done the day before. His tone was soft and pleased like a purr, and I guess he meant for his words to sound gentle, maybe even caring, but I'd never felt so *patronized*.

"No." I tried to sound brave, but my voice came out as a squeak.

He shook his head. "Zeyar is always doing things like that. He likes to bully anyone he can. He's a bitter old man, and he knows he'll advance no further. He has no family connections. Don't pay attention to what he says, and if he hurts you again, come to me."

I nodded and swallowed hard. Xian reached for the tray and carried it to his bed. He perched on the edge of the mattress and lifted a pear to his lips. The sound the fruit made when he bit into it—like a wet kiss—made my whole body shiver. My knees shook with hunger.

Xian patted the bed next to him. "Come sit here. If you're going to work for me, then you have to eat to keep your strength up. We have a busy day today. I know you can't speak my language, but can you write in Thim?"

I considered his question as I sat and tentatively plucked a dumpling from the plate. It still steamed, and the heat of it burned my fingers and tongue. I swallowed it whole rather than spit it out, relishing the feel of something solid trudging down my throat. Should I say that I couldn't write as well? Would he share more of his secrets, then? He already thought I didn't know his language, but as a temple servant, surely I'd have been taught to write at least in my own tongue. Was this a test? I wondered what he already knew about the monks and their customs.

"I can. In Thim," I said and popped another dumpling into my mouth in case the answer was wrong. If he kicked me out, at least I wouldn't be starving when the stewards hauled me to the dungeons.

"Well?"

"Well enough. They teach us here."

He smiled. "Good, you can assist me today. I'll need someone to explain a few words as well, no doubt." His blue-green eyes scrutinized mine. "To explain in private, where no one else will listen."

"Fine," I agreed and selected a pear for myself. As I filled my stomach, I could feel myself relaxing. The task would be easy—and since I knew his language, I could choose metaphors he'd understand without being too obvious. I felt a certain glow of pride. He was going to trust me with secrets already. Maybe I wouldn't fail as a spy after all.

"Was it hard, to leave your family and come here?"

His question made me stop midchew. I didn't know if it was true for all the monks, but for me, any memories of my own family were a haze. Sometimes I remembered sensations—like the feeling of having someone's arms around me while I slept with my face pressed into a threadbare sheet, or the texture of a bearded kiss on my forehead.

Other times I would get flashes of memory that almost didn't seem to belong to me, like they came from Katala or another being altogether.

"I barely remember them," I said.

"That must be really hard."

I shrugged. "You can't miss what you don't remember."

A dull pulse in my stomach and throat told me that was a lie: you could.

Xian bit into a dumpling, chewing carefully, studying me again. "I don't understand it—how so many families can send their children away forever to these temples."

"It's an honor to serve the Ghungza." Trying not to sound bitter, I rattled off what Mistress Lhamo had repeated day after day as we all clustered around her, legs folded and tingling on our meditation mats. That was the opinion that the academy forced on all of us. I assumed it was the same in the monasteries and nunneries across the country.

Here in Thim, it was an honor to be abandoned.

He shrugged, then rolled his eyes a little and grinned. "So it is."

A strange, warm feeling blossomed in my chest. We sat in near silence, finishing off the remains of the food on the tray.

Xian burped and stretched out across the bed. His shirt lifted, revealing the taut muscles underneath and the slight bulge of his full stomach. I looked down and played with the hem of my cloak. Like Pharo, his body was muscular and strong in a way mine wasn't, but he wasn't bulky. Tight, lean tendons ran along his thick arms and flexed. Blushing, I looked away and picked at the bedspread.

"Commander, sir." The steward's voice carried through the thick door. He spoke his own language this time, and I tried not to look interested. "None of them will speak to us in the refectory."

Xian sighed. He pulled his boots out from under the bed and then gestured to the tray. "Take this back to the kitchens and then tidy the room. Come straight back and then don't leave. I may send for you in a while."

Without waiting for me to answer, he stumbled over my pallet and left the room, then yanked the door tight behind him. I heard the mumble of voices as they walked down the hall but couldn't make out anything the steward said. I snatched up the tray and tiptoed to the door. The stone hall had an echo, but if I followed them at a distance, I could listen to what they said....

But as I left the chambers, the maze of halls and doors overwhelmed me. Looking at the crumbs and remains left on the tray, I realized I didn't even know where the kitchen was. Best to look now, rather than risk trying to follow Xian and being caught out of the rooms later. The questions he'd asked me about my life and family all sounded genuine, but I'd seen how easily he slit Kalx's throat. He was cruel.

Turning a corner, I nearly tripped over Pharo. He knelt and scrubbed, his hands peeling and weeping even more than the day before. Guilt nibbled at me. From the color of the water in the bucket, he'd been cleaning for some time, while I slept late and ate better than either of us had since before the siege. Now I wished I'd thought to save a dumpling or a peach for him.

Pharo sat back on his haunches and tossed the rag aside. "Are you okay?" he whispered. "I've been so worried. When I brought the boy back into the hospital ward, I saw Kalx's body…. After that, I imagined all kinds of things that sick bastard might do to you."

I shrugged. I couldn't bring myself to tell Pharo how well I'd eaten and slept. "Nothing bad. I've just been cleaning mostly."

"And watching them feast like kings." His eyes swept over the tray in my hands. Then he seemed to notice my clothes. "At least they gave you something else to wear."

"Yeah." I tugged at the tunic's hem. I didn't like the square, masculine fit. If I'd had my choice today, I would have chosen a wool dress.

Pharo spat in the bucket. "They had us all in the refectory. Asking questions. One of their men was murdered. All they found was a hand."

I swallowed and traced the cobblestones with my toe. "A hand?"

Pharo nodded. Hesitating, he scooted back so he could peer around the corner to make sure no one was listening, before lowering his voice to a whisper. "Pretty gruesome from the sounds of it. I think the rebel forces have made it up to the mountains, but Ugyen said the attack sounds like a wild animal, maybe a wolf pack or something. I haven't been able to connect to see if my wolf knows. Too dangerous right now with all of them watching us so closely."

"They don't believe it was animals?" The tray shook in my hands, and dizziness made my knees weak. I wasn't ready to tell Pharo about Katala yet. I knew what he was like. If he thought I was already instructing her, he would call Faern and try to do the same. His wolf wasn't lethal anymore.

"Well, they don't believe it was random. I don't know what else they think." He climbed stiffly to his feet and took the tray from my quivering hands before I dropped it. "Is he expecting you back?"

"He's gone out."

Pharo's eyes widened. He balanced the tray on one large hand and shoved me with the other. "He's gone out and left you to the room by yourself? What are you waiting for? Search it. He's a commander. He's bound to have all kinds of information. Maps! Papers! Maybe even instruction letters from their general. Maybe they have an idea where the rebel camp is—we could go meet them and get out of this hell pit."

"Do you really think the rebels have made it this far?" I knew that others had escaped before us, but we were never told who or how to contact them. It was too dangerous for the instructors to give us information. If we were questioned or tortured, they wanted to be sure we couldn't reveal their plans. Mistress Lhamo had instructed us to wait at the monastery until the rebels found us, not seek them out on our own.

A lump formed in my throat. When the invasion began, our instructors had thought we would have more time. We had never predicted how quickly the Myeik army could storm our capitol. I wondered what was left of Jakar and tried to imagine the proud Dzong still standing... but all I could picture was a pile of charred bricks and the toppled bronze statue of Ghungza, lips fusing in an ugly, half-melted smile.

"Probably not. Who knows?" The excitement in his eyes flickered and dimmed. He tucked his hands behind his back.

"I'll look," I said, hoping to see his face brighten again. "There's bound to be something."

Relieved that I didn't have to hunt for the kitchens, I turned and made my way back to Xian's suite. Of course Pharo had thought to look for letters, information, anything. He'd always been top of our class and brave—so much braver than me. I wished Xian had chosen him instead.

I slipped back into the room and hastily tidied the space. I threw Xian's discarded clothes under the bed to deal with them later and brushed dirt under the discarded tapestries with my foot. I couldn't imagine what "secrets" Xian might hide, since his own army had exiled him to a monastery to babysit the wounded, but Pharo was right. He could have hidden something, and I might not get this chance again.

When they took over his suite, the Myeik army emptied all of the abbot's belongings. The room's few drawers hung ajar and empty. Someone had chipped the woodwork in the carved wardrobe. Other than the pile of old clothes I'd kicked under the bed, Xian kept only a worn leather saddle in the corner of the room.

I knelt on the floor next to it and ran my fingers over the rough seat. A film of dirt and crumbled leaves covered the suede panels. The saddle looked as if it hadn't been cleaned for weeks, and I wondered why Xian wouldn't have given it to the stewards after his last ride. Looking more closely, I made out old spiral patterns and images of dragons. I wiped the dragon's eyes clean, and tiny emeralds winked at me. Once, this saddle would have been a prize.

Caught in the fold beneath the cantle and the stirrup leather, a small slip of paper was wedged into the metal brace. I tried to tease open the hinge, but years of hard use and ill-keeping made the saddle stiff and unyielding. The hinge stuck in place. I braced myself on my elbow and tried to pull the paper through without ripping it in the process.

"What are you doing?"

My head whipped around. The steward stood looking in at me from the other side of the doorway.

"Trying to clean," I offered and hoped he didn't see the way my fingers shook as I lowered them to rest on my knees. "This saddle is filthy."

Zeyar nodded, pressing his lips together. "Well, in the future, don't touch the commander's personal things unless he specifically tells you to. Xian can be touchy about that. That saddle is very old and very special to him. As I understand, his mother gave it to him. Anyway, you're wanted. Come with me."

He crooked a finger, summoning me like a pet dog. Fear made my knees lock as I tried to climb to my feet.

A frozen wind blew through the hall, cold against the bare skin of my shaved head. I missed the warmth of my hair and the way I could let it hang in front of my eyes like a shield, hiding emotion. My throat felt dry, and I was glad Zeyar didn't seem to expect me to speak.

He took me by the bicep and pulled me quickly down the corridor without even pausing to close the door. A sudden thought made my breath stick in my chest... what if Xian hadn't even sent for me? What if this man was taking me of his own accord? Was I allowed to defend myself?

I pulled up short, yanking my arm out of his grasp. "How do I know you're not lying to me?"

Zeyar growled. He snatched my earlobe instead, and I instantly regretted testing him. "I don't have time for this. The commander orders, we obey."

Digging his nails in harder, he pulled me down a flight of steps into the basement of the monastery. The rush of fear inside me spiked Katala's attention, and a headache began to pound at my temple, so intense it nearly forced me to my knees. I clutched my stomach, but Zeyar didn't slow. Nausea overcame me as we descended deeper into the basement, and the taste of blood filled my mouth. I stopped again, bracing myself on the stone wall.

"Oh for fuck's sake." The steward released my ear and grabbed me by the collar instead. He slapped my face. "It's not you we're questioning. Pull yourself together."

"Don't touch what doesn't belong to you." Xian's voice came out flat and cold. He sounded so much older outside the abbot's rooms. I looked down at him with relief, even as part of my brain rebelled at being described as a belonging.

"Yes sir, Commander." The steward straightened himself and pushed me down the last few stairs.

Falling at his feet, I stared up at Xian. He had stripped to the waist, and blood dripped down his muscular torso. A gold chain hung from his neck, bearing a ruby pendant. His palms and fingers were also covered in red. Something like panic rose in my throat. He was hurt.

"What happened?" I asked. "Did you get in a fight?"

Behind me, Zeyar started laughing.

"Come on," Xian said. He ignored my question and looked to Zeyar. "Go back up the stairs and guard the level. Make sure no one else comes down. Even my personal guards."

When the steward had gone, Xian cupped my face with his bloody hand. My headache nearly blinded me. Blood always stirred Katala into a frenzy. She smelled violence through me as easily as a hound catching the scent of a boar. "What you will see may disturb you. I trust you... well, it doesn't matter who of your own that you tell. Gossip with the monks all you like if you trust them to stay silent around my men. But know that if you tell anything he says to my own soldiers, I will find out."

It was unnerving, the way he stroked my cheek and threatened me at the same time.

Xian led me deep into the catacombs. My eyes took too long to adjust, but I could hear the sounds of water crawling down the walls and of someone weeping.

Ugyen sat bound to a chair in the center of the room. His lip bled, and the flesh under his eyes was bruised and turning black. A line of red extended down from his collarbone to just below his navel. It was so straight and perfect that it looked like a tattoo made by a skilled artist, but it glistened wet.

Xian pulled his dagger out of its scabbard. He placed the tip against Ugyen's throat. "Before his death, Master Leyu said, 'She sent them to Ugyen.' Tell me again, was he talking about you?"

My whole body began to shake. Master Leyu was the name of our mathematics tutor, and he was close to Mistress Lhamo. I tried to take a breath—Leyu and Ugyen were common names.

Xian could be talking about any person from the city, a member of the infantry perhaps, or the son of a wealthy nobleman.

"No," said Ugyen without a trace of fear. It was wrong, so, so wrong that he could sound so calm in his position, when ants crawled up and down my back.

"Ugyen is a common name here," I blurted out.

Xian scowled at me, then gestured to a bench by the wall. "There is parchment there on the bench. You will take a transcription. If he reveals something important, I want to be the one to pass the information on."

Nodding, I slunk to the bench. Ugyen pressed his lips together and gave me the smallest of nods. I could have sworn that he was promising me his silence.

"One of my men is dead," Xian hissed. He lowered his face to look Ugyen in the eyes. My fingers shook so hard I almost couldn't lift the quill. "We found his hand, and all the surgeons say it was an animal."

Ugyen gave him a mocking shrug. "Maybe it was, Commander... sir."

"Your novices, as young as seven, walk through the forests here, alone and barefoot with no weapons. None of them have ever seen a wolf or a great cat. Tell me, why would a simple creature attack an armed adult man and leave his horse unharmed, when there are twenty children about?"

"How can I explain how an animal acts?"

"When I cut you before, you said there had been a faelg? What does it have to do with it all?" When Ugyen shut his lips, Xian looked to me. There was a mad sparkle in his eyes, determination and something else, something more frightening. It might have been pleasure. "This is why you are here. What is a faelg?"

I didn't understand why it was important that we keep the secret of the faelg. Why did it matter if they knew what happened to us? Xian's fist collided with Ugyen's stomach, and still the monk stayed silent. If he didn't want to tell, there was a reason. I had to play along.

I bit my lip. "Someone who trained to be a wizard and didn't make it... they were not good enough. Could not complete the training or failed their final set of trials."

The Myeik already thought of the inhabitors as wizards, so why not encourage Xian down that path? The commander turned away from Ugyen to stare at me instead.

From the monk's bloody smile, I knew I was right to lie.

Xian's shoulders relaxed. "See, this is why I needed someone who understands your language and your culture. And one who knows they have everything to gain by allying themself with me." He spat at Ugyen. Gray mucus slithered down the old monk's chin, but still he didn't flinch. "So there was a failed wizard here? If he failed, why do I care? If he did not complete the tests, then he cannot hope to control such a thing as a wolf."

I pressed my hand to my temple. The headache had faded to a dull pulse, but I could almost feel Katala just waiting. It was the calm before the storm, like those moments she spent hiding in the tall grass, waiting as her prey wandered into position.

Xian punched Ugyen again, and I struggled to reconcile this creature of hate with the boy who had fed me and asked about my family. I'd given him an answer, so why continue? He growled and he pointed toward the pen and inkwell. Sighing, I picked them up and rested the writing tablet against my knees. Together the three of us settled into a dance: punch, question, denial, all accompanied by the furious tempo of my quill twisting across the rice sheet.

LATER THAT night, I prepared a bath by pouring boiling water into a tub of melted snow. The tub filled and steamed as the waters mixed together. I added the salts the steward had given me and inhaled the scents of lavender and pepper. After uncorking a small vial made of delicately twisted green glass, I twirled jasmine oil into the water. Then I plunged my forearms into the bath and splashed my face, trying in vain to wash away some of the cowardice.

Xian tossed his bloodstained trousers onto the floor and stepped into the tub of lukewarm water. Belatedly, I looked away while he undressed, and focused on the calming scents of the oils instead. I didn't trust myself to make eye contact with him. Not after what I'd just seen. I needed time to come back to myself. He sank into the water, sighing and closing his bright eyes. When he snapped his fingers, as imperious as a little emperor, I pulled the cork out of the silver bottle containing the hair oil and poured it down his scalp. Xian's bath oils and salts probably cost more than the grain to feed this whole monastery through a winter. The water turned pink as Ugyen's blood dripped down Xian's back.

Sometimes, back at the academy, a traveling bard would stop to tell us stories. We each paid him a silver piece, and he would sing to us. Pausing between bars of music played on a long flute, he had told us about heroines and heroes whose loyalty, goodness, and bravery shone. We had learned about the princess who saved her kingdom, her beauty the envy of the civilized world. And Pharo used to clap his hands with delight when the bard sang about the warrior king who rescued damsels and fought off sea monsters, his eyes as black and glossy as midnight.

Xian had none of the heroes' qualities.

He was vicious, sadistic, and unreadable—qualities of the villains in all the bards' tales. I wouldn't be safe until he and his men were far away. None of us would be. But still, a small part of me longed to reach out and touch him, to stroke his back and ignore the cruelty that festered inside him. He reached back and scrubbed his shoulders with a soft green cloth. My fingers twitched at my sides.

CHAPTER 5

I LEFT him to soak, blaming the heat rising to my face on the water's steam and the stress of the interrogation. Xian tilted his head back and closed his eyes. I scurried to a far corner of the room, pressing my cheek against the cold glass of the window. The dull pulse in my temple began to race, the pain almost blinding again. I gritted my teeth and willed my breathing to slow down. Katala sensed that something had changed. My fear had transformed into another feeling, equally powerful but different, and it intrigued her.

I couldn't be feeling lust, although all these symptoms fit. But maybe it was normal? Maybe the calm lull after the violence I'd recorded was playing with my head. Back at the academy, Mistress Lhamo often talked about battle fever in our history classes. For all I knew, it could be Katala and her sudden foray into man slaying who was influencing me, rather than the other way around.

I picked one of the tapestries off the floor and shook the dust from it. It depicted one of Thim's founders aboard a black stallion. He wound his way through the mountains accompanied by a white leopard that trotted behind the horse's heels. Whether the founder had been an inhabitor or not, I didn't know. Many of our nobles chose to have themselves painted as if they were. The texture of the lotus fibers was familiar, soothing. Lifting it to my face, I breathed in the smell of the home I should have forgotten—stale, but lingering deep within the fibers, obscured by layers of smoke and incense, like a scented palimpsest.

"What are you doing?" Xian stood behind me, a towel loosely tied around his waist. Water pooled at his feet. "We took those down for a reason. They show Jakar's victories. They were all over the temple. We stripped them down, and now we walk on them where the monks can see."

"These are expensive," I stammered. "The fibers... they take years to grow, mature, and spin. You should keep them to sell."

He snorted, then took the tapestry from me and folded it. "I suppose some collector somewhere might want them. The things they show are part of history now anyway."

I looked into his eyes and saw some of that same mocking cruelty that had been there when he tortured Ugyen. His hands went to his hips. My mouth felt dry and too full of emotion to form words. I couldn't bring myself to challenge him, so I glared down at my feet instead, fingers curling into fists.

"In a generation, these will be like looking at pictures from a fairy story." Xian laughed and pushed the tapestry into my chest. "Here, keep this one. My gift to you. You performed well today. I could tell you were afraid, but your transcription is very clear."

I held the tapestry to my body like a blanket. I felt torn, yet again, between gratitude and hate. I knew the gift meant nothing to him, but I'd never owned anything that reminded me so acutely of the home I'd left behind.

Someone knocked on the door. Xian scowled. He pulled the towel tighter around his waist. "I didn't call for anyone."

He gestured toward the door and seated himself on his bed. He sat straight, almost rigidly, and schooled his mouth into an emotionless frown. It amazed me that someone could look so poised and in control while dripping wet and clad only in a gray towel.

Still clutching the tapestry, I opened the door, expecting the steward with Xian's dinner tray or a message from the camp. Instead, a towering woman stood on the doorstep with a letter clutched in her gloved hand. She was draped in furs, with frost coating her eyelashes. Zeyar and two other soldiers hovered behind her. They were exchanging glances. One of them fiddled with the hem of his jersey. Whoever this person was, if she made Zeyar nervous, I didn't want to be around her, but I remained frozen in the doorway, unsure whether to usher them inside or warn Xian.

"Well?" Xian asked. "Show them in."

"Are you sure? It's not just—"

"Don't question me." His voice came out like nails. I cringed. "Show them in."

I opened the door wider and stepped aside. A freezing gust of wind blew in with the visitor, but Xian didn't even flinch. The two soldiers remained in the hall. I paused a moment to give them another chance to enter and then shut the door with a satisfying snap in Zeyar's face.

The stranger's eyes swept over Xian's attire, but she didn't comment. When she spoke, her voice was so rough from the cold I struggled to understand her words. "I'm sorry to disturb you so late. But I've just arrived from the main camp, and I wanted to come to you first." She looked to me. "Shouldn't you send him out?"

"They," Xian said with pointed emphasis, "don't understand our language. They're just a temple servant that I picked up when we got here."

The woman nodded and began to strip off her gloves and furs. I scurried forward to catch a white sable before it hit the floor. None of the furs were tailored or styled. As she peeled them off, I collected the skins of rare animals from across the world until, last of all, she unwound the orange-and-black pelt of a tiger from around her neck. My desire to run from the room grew stronger.

"General Liu is worried," the messenger said, collapsing into a chair opposite the bed as Xian's brows furrowed. "She says that when we took the Dzong and the academy, many of the officials and instructors we expected to find inside were missing. We knew that some would escape, of course, or die in the siege, but we didn't think it would be so many. When we stormed the academy, only three were alive. We found bodies—none of them marked, none of them starved—they just looked as though they drifted off to sleep and never woke. But there weren't enough, and none of them were young."

Hope surged inside me. Pharo and I weren't alone. The army hadn't found any of the others who made it out. They would contact us soon. I knew they would. Then I could get away from Xian and this dangerous game of deception.

Xian stroked the stubble around his chin. "Does General Liu think they're here? In the mountains? The Thim have always relied on these mountains to protect them."

The messenger shrugged and wiped tears of melting ice from her cheeks. "She thinks they are everywhere."

Xian shuddered. "That's what the peasants say. I heard that much before I left the city."

"We know the academy trains the military special forces, but no one really knows what they do. Even the officials at the Dzong don't know everything. The peasants say they turn into animals, that they can start fires with a word and that their bodies melt into rivers and become water. They're legends as much as soldiers."

I held the tapestry to my face and tried to hide a proud smile. Our magic was ancient and little understood outside the academy. Even after years of study and practice, I barely understood the power I wielded. The peasants thought we could do anything and that we were immortal. The mystery surrounding the academy protected us—had done for a thousand years.

"One of my men was attacked by a wild animal. Killed. I don't believe it was random," Xian said.

The visitor nodded. "It's happened elsewhere also. General Liu does not think it is random either. In one outpost, a sentry was trampled to death by a takin. An onlooker said he didn't provoke the beast and there was no calf. Have you ever heard of such a thing? They're grazers... peaceful."

"Here it was something bigger. I think a wolf, maybe a male snow leopard. But the monks send baby novices alone into the woods to collect tree sap... no one has ever been attacked here. Not in the thousand years of this place's history as far as anyone could say. I asked all the novices in the hall."

"The general is sending more forces here. We will use this place as an outpost to comb the mountains. Just soldiers, no officers. They'll be under your command, of course." The messenger rubbed the back of her head and grinned. "She was livid, you know. That even from a monastery in the middle of nowhere, your family still manages to be in the middle of things."

Xian laughed, then stood and sighed. "And you, Chen? Will you be returning to the city?"

The woman shrugged as she handed the letter over to Xian. "I'll be staying to aid you. I'm the best tracker we have in the army. If anyone can find these wizards hiding as animals in the woods, it will be me. It's quite a task they're giving you. But your father must have thought you'd be up to it when he enrolled you."

"Tashi, go make us some tea," Xian said, breaking my concentration on their words. He clapped Chen on the shoulder. "Excuse me for a moment. It's going to be a long night, and I'd rather get dressed."

AFTER A search, I found Pharo in the kitchens. He sat warming himself by the cook fire and drinking thick soup from a ladle. When he saw me, he lifted the hem of his blanket and patted the ground beside him. "Don't like sleeping in the dorms without you there. I've never had a room to myself. It's cold, and the quiet makes it hard to sleep. I don't know how these monks get by."

I sat on the earth and slid under the blanket next to him. Then rested my head on his shoulder. Years ago, I'd been in love with Pharo. He was my first crush. I was drawn to his strength and easy popularity, following him around the academy like a stray pup, basking in whatever attention he'd give me. Pharo had been in love with a girl in our class—a beautiful, lively girl who dyed turquoise streaks in her dark hair and used to sing for all of us in the dinner hall. Back then, I'd envied everything about her. I'd wanted her smile and her body's softness. I wanted Pharo's eyes to light up when he saw me.

In our fifth year, she had performed at the winter ceremonies in front of the ministers from the Dzong. We listened to her sing, and I still remember how Pharo's eyes went glassy with awe. Jealousy had beaten in my breast, as furiously as the tempo of the drum. She reached a crescendo, her ethereal voice wavering with emotion. The whole room sat forward on their benches, listening to each tremoring note as it echoed around the chamber.

Then her voice cracked. Her knees buckled. And her eyes died.

She was bonded to a finch and cursed to sing brightly, but not for very long. Pharo had closed his eyes, squeezed my fingers under the table, and at thirteen, we both learned that it wasn't safe to love anyone.

Pharo never talked about having a crush again. I kept my own feelings buried deep.

"There's a messenger," I said without lifting my head. "She came up from Jakar."

Pharo fished out another ladle of the soup and pressed it to my lips. "What did she say?"

Finally, I allowed my face to split into a smile. "They escaped. The other inhabitors. Not everyone, but lots did. They didn't find any initiates."

Pharo let out a low breath. Neither of us said anything for a moment. We just let the relief swaddle us.

"There's more," I said. "They're sending more men up. They think rebels killed that man, and they want Xian to find them. The messenger they sent is some kind of tracking expert."

"Xian? You're on a first-name basis with that monster commander now?" Trust Pharo to skip right over everything else I'd said.

"It's what he told me to call him," I snapped. "I don't want to mess up when I'm with him."

He made a gagging noise in the back of his throat. "They still think the rebels are responsible for that sentry's death. If they're from the academy, that tracker will never find them."

I looked into the fire. I couldn't keep the secret from him any longer. I whispered, "It was Katala."

Pharo turned toward me, gripping me by both shoulders. His eyes were wide and dilated with excitement. "Katala—you—she killed that sentry?"

Bitterness filled my mouth: the ghost taste of salt, iron, and frozen flesh. I nodded. "She dragged the body into her den. She was trying to get my attention all day… I could barely even see because of the headache… she was really proud."

"Too right." Pharo spooned another ladle of soup into his mouth. "Aren't you proud of her? She killed one of them, probably identified him using your memories like all the ancient texts say. So, you did something for our side."

I swallowed. "It just doesn't feel great, you know? Killing someone like that. Or being responsible for it. I know we trained for this, but it just… he was a person, and it wasn't a battle. No one was coming after me."

Pharo's eyes narrowed, and he jabbed his finger into my chest. "All those people who died in the siege? They were people. They were our friends. Remember all the people we saw tossed over the walls? They weren't even soldiers. They were just normal people who starved to death. Don't let this commander make you his pet. Most of us never get the chance to be useful. We just train and train, hoping that one day the Dzong might call for our specific skill like they did during the Great Wars… and die before we even hit twenty. Katala has the right idea. You have to help her do it again."

My stomach flipped over. The idea of helping Katala mark her human prey made me sick and a little bit excited at the same time. I wanted to matter, but I wasn't sure I was ready.

"Maybe Faern and I can help…." His voice trailed off, and he looked at his feet instead of me.

"You'll die," I whispered. My hand went to my throat. He was my only friend now that Kalx was gone and the closest thing to family I had left. "Faern is old and getting slow. You'll die."

"I'll matter. And I'm going to die anyway. Soon. I can feel it." His eyes brimmed, and I couldn't look at him. Pharo didn't cry.

I brushed his blanket off and got to my feet. Suddenly, the way our shoulders touched overwhelmed me. The gentle heat burned like hot ash. "I have tea to make. I should get back. He'll notice if I'm away too long."

Pharo nodded. He toyed with the hem of the blanket and lay down in the space I'd vacated. He drew the blanket over his shoulders and side. Curled up by the fire like that, with his muscle concealed by the ragged cloth, he looked like a forgotten old dog: tired, worn, and sad.

AT MIDNIGHT, Chen took her leave and Xian crawled into bed to rest. I lay on top of my blankets, listening as his breathing evened and his body stilled. Then I tiptoed to the privy and sealed myself inside.

Chen planned to patrol. She wanted to get a sense of the land at night, when all the humans were asleep. Then she could be alone in the blistering cold and quiet of the mountains, to listen, to watch. And while she stalked the night on her clumsy human feet, Katala and I would stalk her. And we would do it better.

My consciousness slipped into the tiger's form. She was stretched out on her cave's floor, middream, snuggling a bone with the rough dimensions of a human femur. In her dreams, she waded through a river, a wriggling trout in her mouth, a pair of cubs splashing at her feet. A feeling of hollowness filled her chest. I tried, too late, to shut the dream from my thoughts. Cats felt desire, I'd learned, but they couldn't truly mourn for what wasn't like we did. But when we shared a body, Katala could feel the effects of my emotions, experience the very human intensity of them in the same way I smelled sweat on the wind through her sensitive nostrils. She stirred, growling in confusion at the pain. The dream died away.

Katala climbed to her feet and stretched out her spine. She extended her paws and dug her massive claws into the frozen earth. I felt weight in her belly again. She wouldn't feel like hunting now, which boded well. I wasn't ready to experience an attack on another person yet, but if she were hungry, then nothing would stop her from hunting. I wasn't sure what I planned to do to Chen once we found her. I didn't want my tiger's instincts to make the decision for me.

Like always, Katala knew what I wanted to see. Padding out into the darkness, she wound down the mountainside like a serpent, slithering through narrow gaps in the icy rock. We crept close to the monastery and crouched low. The birds slept, and even the kitchen lights were dimmed. The only noise I could hear was the steady breath of the wind as it moved through the pine trees.

Something flickered at the edge of my vision. Katala's whole body pivoted. She tucked her tail, and her legs gathered to pounce or run. A lone deer froze in the clearing. She grazed on a lush patch of half-frozen ferns, but when she smelled Katala's faint scent and felt the golden tiger's eyes on her, she bounded away without a sound.

At the academy, Mistress Lhamo had once told us that it wasn't uncommon for the animals to fall asleep when the inhabitor connected with them. For some species, the sense of dual consciousness was too much, and they preferred to avoid the unknown by hiding in dream worlds of their own making. Katala never shied away. I was grateful for that because stalking, creeping, hunting, and killing were far outside the realm of anything I'd been trained to do. And as long as it was her doing the killing, I could cling to the idea that I was still just a spy, not a murderer. Maybe I was the one who drifted into a dream whenever we connected.

A stick snapped just meters away from us. Panic punched through me like an arrow to the chest. It couldn't be possible. Chen could not have found us already. Squinting in the direction of the sound, I could make out the barest whisper of white fur moving amongst the trees.

The specter disappeared behind a wall of mist and pine. Katala sniffed at the wind, trying to catch the ghost's scent.

Panting, a large gray-and-white wolf stumbled into the clearing. He had eyes of pure silver. I recognized Pharo's wolf immediately. Faern licked his lips and sat. His tail thumped the ground like an oversized puppy's. When his lips curled back in a toothy smile, I smelled the aging rot in his gums. The wolf rolled over on his back and exposed his belly to the tiger.

Katala went to him and butted her head against his back. The wolf whined and struggled to his feet. Attacking an armed man would be a death sentence for the old wolf and the inhabitor who shared a soul with him. I wasn't ready to lose Pharo. Not yet. Not ever.

I wanted to stay with Faern, to make sure that he and Pharo didn't rush headlong at an armed sentry or gnaw their way into a tent of sleeping men—or worse still, run into Chen as she hunted.

But Katala turned away, and a second later we were vertical. Her claws dug into pine bark, and she propelled us up the tree trunk. Settling atop a high branch, she watched Faern from below, ignoring his whimpers. The wolf tucked his tail and trotted away through the trees.

From the height of the pine, I could see over the monastery walls and survey the woods for a mile all around it. With Katala's sharp senses, I could make out individual needles on the trees, hear a monk's boots crunch through the snow on his way to the privy. For her, the darkness illuminated everything.

A flicker of orange appeared in the clearing below us. I squinted down as Chen's dawn-embossed shadow fell across the frosted earth. She grunted with effort, dragging something behind her. At first all I could see was a flash of white fur. I smelled blood, human and something else, a blood rich with meat, dense and sweet. I sniffed the air again. There was an aftertaste in the blood, something putrid and sour, like the mold that grows on bread. Katala's whole body went rigid with anticipation.

Groaning and wiping his brow, Chen marched past us. Covered by her furs, she looked almost like a patchwork bear. She pulled the bleeding carcass of a snow leopard behind her. The animal's eyes were vacant, and its huge paws trailed uselessly, claws still extended.

Snow leopards were as elusive as they were vicious. When I was a child, my mother used to sing about the white devils in the mountains that came down from their lairs to eat naughty children before the winter solstice feasts. These were creatures that melted into the forest like ghosts, who killed, lived, and died without a trace. And this woman had found one.

I shut my eyes, disconnecting from Katala. The metal rain hit my skin like the ends of a whip. I knelt up and vomited down the privy's long tunnel. How long before she dragged Faern's body back to her military hut for skinning? Could she kill Katala? My tiger weighed three times more than that leopard, but she'd done that alone. With a group of soldiers like the ones following her from Jakar, maybe she could kill a golden tiger. I imagined Katala's skin, carefully scraped from her body, wrapped around Chen's shoulders. At least if that happened, I would never see it.

Breath ragged, I gripped the edge of the privy seat, knuckles turning white with anger. The Myeik tracker was not going to wear our skins around her neck. I had a tiger's senses and teeth at my disposal. I would make sure that all of us lived.

CHAPTER 6

"IT'S A delicacy in my country," Xian said, reaching into the woven basket for a sticky honey-and-sesame-covered rib. "Try it. It's delicious. Trust me. I can't believe Chen found this on her first night here. That woman is legendary."

Despite the sweet scent wafting out of the basket, my stomach turned over. "I'm not very well this morning," I stammered. "I'm honored, but it would be wasted on me today."

Xian shrugged and ripped a shred of fat-laden meat from the bone with his teeth. He smacked his lips together. "Must be a good luck omen. Hopefully this is the beast that killed that what's-his-name's sentry. I'll have to patrol today. Maybe you should come with me. The beasts must favor the monks."

The killings wouldn't stop. I knew Katala well enough to know she wouldn't give up her dangerous new game.

I swallowed and squeaked out, "Is it safe? To be outside?"

He scowled, studying my face until I dropped my gaze to the blankets. For all their brightness, his eyes gave away nothing. Then he reached out and patted my cheek like a dog. "Don't worry, little Tashi. Nothing's going to eat you while you're with me."

The way he patronized me stung, but I pushed the conversation forward anyway. Whether I liked it or not, I needed him to open up to me. I had to keep the hope that there were others from the academy, and when Pharo and I found them, closeness with Xian would give me something to report. My reports could make the difference between defeating an entire regiment or not.

Xian scooted close to me, near enough for me to feel the prickle of warmth from his thigh against mine. Licking my lips, I gestured to the tray. "Do you eat a lot of game then? In your home?"

He rubbed the back of his head. "I'm from the Silay Lakes. There's not much there other than fish and birds. When we catch something else with more substance to the meat, we eat it."

I racked my brain for long-forgotten knowledge about that region in Myeik but came up blank. I could hear Master Leyu's monotone voice rattling off snippets of their history. But when he described our southern neighbors, I never paid much attention. His voice lulled in the background of another memory, of Kalx showing me how to fold paper tigers out of rice sheets. Neither of us saw the point in paying attention. Not then. Not when everything seemed so safe.

The invasion seemed to come out of nowhere, and no one at the Dzong expected it. The Myeik invaded without warning. New languages had always come easily to me, but why remember history when we hadn't had a war in centuries? The inhabitors who had spied on the Myeik camps reported that the lack of fertile soil and laborers in their country had pushed them over the mountains toward us. They'd struggled for decades before invading, and shielded by our ignorance and the mountains, we'd never known or cared. Everyone felt that the snow-capped peaks that stretched a hundred miles deep served as our geological fortress. We'd never imagined the war machines the Myeik were building.

I cursed myself. I had been complacent. I had been naïve. I was just doing what all the inhabitors did then, and enjoying the experience of life for as long as I got to live it. We all tried to trick ourselves into thinking that the life we had was real and that time belonged to us.

"I don't remember much from outside the monastery," I said, dragging myself out of the memories and turning to look at him. "Tell me about your home."

Xian looked out the frosted window. He chewed his lip, and for a minute, I allowed myself to believe that he might feel sadness. Then he turned to me with a grin on his face but hollowness in his eyes. "It's warm, and we build on the water. In the lakes region, most people build houses up on stilts and use canoes or barges to go between. Our cities are huge.... Tha-Le has over a million people, all living and working on the water. At the center, there is a man-made island where some of the nobles live. My family lives there."

I tried to picture it, a country with more people clustered in a single city than in the whole of our country, a city built without foundations. "Don't they flood?" I asked. "The houses?"

Xian shook his head. "We build the platforms high enough that the houses stay above the water level even in the rainy season. The water is calm. We don't have storms like you do here. We get one lightning storm a year, always on the same day. The gods send it to remind us that they're still watching." He groaned and pressed his hand to his forehead. "May the eleventh. And on that day, next year, I lose my freedom to roam, forever."

My eyebrows rose. Here I was, stuck serving him, and he was talking about losing his freedom.

He saw my expression and laughed. "I know what you're thinking. And I guess you're right to think it. But in a year, I get married. I've never met her."

In Thim, forced marriages violated all our religious teachings. Love was not a commodity we sold and exchanged for politics. A few times a year, Mistress Lhamo would take us to the public square on Retribution Days. Dressed in our brilliant yellow processional robes, we followed her like a troop of ducklings. Once I saw a man's hand cut off for trying to pawn his daughter to a local merchant. Xian talked about it like it was normal.

"Doesn't that... bother you?"

"Oh, it's not the marriage part that'll be so bad. But after, it means I have to settle. Have to produce an heir, build my own house. If we're lucky, we might become friends. But either way, after we have a baby or four, I can ignore her forever and she can ignore me. It's true... some of what you hear... in Myeik, most of us have lovers. They give us the care our spouses never will."

"Why marry at all, then?"

Xian shrugged. "It seals the dynasties together. Keeps the peace. Means that all the generals, senators... we're all family in some branch or another." He cleared his throat and picked at the quilt on the bed.

"It seems like a sad way to live. If you don't love them, why can't you say no?"

"It's my duty," he said. "We believe in family before everything."

As my family had abandoned me soon after I learned to walk, I had a hard time imagining a world where family mattered so much. Then, I supposed that we were bound to service of the Ghungza and maybe the two things—and the duty that compelled us—weren't so different after all.

LATER THAT afternoon, Xian went to meet Chen and the stewards brought me a fresh set of clothes. I dressed and paced the room, unsure of what to do or where to go until Xian came back. Pain throbbed in my head, growing stronger and more insistent the more time passed. I sat against the wall, banging my head back against the stones to quiet Katala's phantom pulse. When the pain became so overwhelming it started to blur my vision, I got up again and went outside in search of Pharo.

Not for the first time, I cursed Katala and her lack of consideration. At the academy, Pharo always used to tease me and say that I should have bonded with a wolf if I wanted sympathy instead of a giant cat. *Cats don't care*, he'd laughed. And even though I knew that wasn't quite true, sometimes I wished a little of Faern's empathetic nature had rubbed off on Katala over the years.

When I stepped out of the door, sunlight warmed my cheeks. The light flickered like a candle behind the mountain peaks, but the heat soothed the sting of the icy wind. I trotted through the courtyard. Black and blue spots formed in my vision from the brightness of the snow and the dizzying, relentless headache that Katala gave me. The cherry tree had bloomed again. Red, pink, and white blossoms scattered on the snow like drops of ink on a perfect canvas. Fragrant, freezing wind blistered my lips.

"Where are you off to in such a hurry?"

I jumped, nearly tripping over a shrub into the snow. Chen heaved herself off the ground beneath the cherry tree. Her nose twitched. I struggled to stand still, imagining that she could smell my guilt.

"On my way to the kitchens." I smoothed the hem of my new tunic and swallowed. "Ma'am."

"I just saw the commander leave for a patrol ride. Not stealing food, are you?" Cocking her head sideways to peer into my face, she reached inside her furs and pulled out a napkin. Thrusting it into my hands, she said, "A piece of sweet bread for some information."

I lifted the corner of the napkin. Inside was a brown loaf stuffed with figs and fresh ginger. I broke off a tiny piece and put it to my lips. A dusting of white sugar snowed over my palm. The sweetness stuck to the roof of my dry mouth. I couldn't imagine what she wanted to know.

The woman scuffed her foot over the frozen earth. Her uncertainty intrigued me. Whatever information she was seeking scared her more than hunting a snow leopard alone. "I only ask these things out of concern for the commander, you understand."

Her accent was thick, and I could tell she wasn't used to our language.

I nodded, stuffing the bread into my mouth so she couldn't take it back.

"How does he seem to you? Agitated? Concerned? Has he had any secret messages? Night visitors? A note perhaps, that you've seen?" Chen pulled her furs tighter around her neck. She glanced at the tree and did not look at me as she said, "The general asks. Things at Xian's home are not well... and she is concerned about his state of mind. Concerned that maybe he should return to Myeik or that he is not processing information here as he should. She gave him a pass to visit his family in the letter I brought with me, but he has declined."

I thought back to the saddle and the note tucked under the leather flap. This woman could make a powerful friend and could protect me if I offended Xian. Chen plucked at a pine needle embedded in one of her furs. I followed her fingers as they moved over the white-and-black spotted pattern—against the white, a drop of red that hadn't been completely cleaned away.

I swallowed. Whatever I needed, she wasn't the protector I wanted.

"I'm sorry. I haven't seen any notes." When Chen's eyes narrowed, I rushed on. "But the commander, he does seem distant. Perhaps he just does not know me very well...."

I let my voice trail off, but the suggestion hovered in the air. Chen snatched at it, her lips parted to reveal her yellow teeth in a sort of grimace-smile. "You'll tell me if you see anything? Hear anything?"

Wind blew through the cherry tree, coating her with blossoms. The effect of those delicate, half-frozen petals clinging to her stinking pelts was grotesque. I wanted to turn away, but I forced myself to look her in the eye.

"Of course," I lied. "Anything I hear. You just want what's best for him. As do I. The monks mistreated me when I was their temple servant. I don't have any loyalty to them."

The tracker looked skyward, and her tongue darted out like a lizard's, catching a falling snowflake. The delicate flake sizzled on her acid kiss. She patted the crossbow strapped to her back. "That's good. Now off to the kitchens with you. I've hunting to do." Winking, she added, "If you snatch something from the kitchens, I'll say it was me."

Chen trudged across the courtyard toward the wall. I turned on my heels and ran, suddenly needing to get as far away from her and her pelts as possible. I looked over my shoulder, and she saluted me before readying her bow and stepping out through the front gate.

The door to the kitchen was ajar and the room empty. Pharo's pot of soup still swung over the fire's ashes, the ladle on the floor pressed against the grate. Ugyen must have been keeping him busy with chores. Trays of sweetmeats and dumplings lay on the counter, dressed with flowers carved from vegetables and ready to be served. I leaned over them and inhaled. I pinched one between my fingers and blew on it before popping it into my mouth. Hot fat dripped down my throat and soothed my aching stomach.

"You know the monks made those." Ugyen had appeared in the doorway. He made no move to approach, just leaned against a polished walking stick he hadn't needed before Xian beat him. His ceremonial staff was nowhere to be seen. "For the soldiers. All their lives these monks have avoided touching the flesh of slaughtered animals. And now they're stuck making treats from pig fat to avoid limping like I do."

The sweetness of the dumpling turned bitter. I wiped my mouth on my sleeve. Ugyen hobbled into the room. Looking me straight in the eye, he demanded, "Where is he?"

"The commander? He's riding out...."

His eyes narrowed. "Don't play the idiot with me." Wincing, he bent down in front of the fireplace and scooped up a handful of soot. He brandished it at me. Little chunks of metal glimmered against the black ash and cobwebs. "Look at this. Where's your friend gone?"

"Have you checked the dormitory?" I asked, bracing my weight on the counter. My voice was calm, but fear rose inside me. I remembered the glimmer in his eye when I'd told Pharo about Katala's attacks. He wanted nothing more than to matter.

Ugyen smacked the back of my head. "Of course I checked there. No one has seen him since yesterday."

A spasm of dizziness passed through me as fear made me weak. It was bad enough that he was using Faern to patrol, but to move his even more vulnerable human body out there with Chen on the hunt.... I fought the urge to retch into the pot on the hearth. "He must be here somewhere... he wouldn't go out there... he *wouldn't.*"

"What do you know that you haven't told me?"

I shrugged. Ugyen could keep secrets—he'd proved that with Xian—but if he knew what Katala had done, then he might stop me... and I wasn't sure I wanted him to. "Nothing.... I just.... He's been so restless. And you're working him to the bone."

Ugyen pursed his lips tight. "I just want him to stay out of sight. I can still protect one of you."

A chink in his perfect armor. "Yeah well, they're hardly noticing any of you, so why not give him some freedom? The Myeik are preoccupied running their hospital and hunting rebels outside these walls. I don't think they even notice what is going on here."

"They've hardly moved any of the wounded here. And the commander doesn't take any interest in the ward preparations." He limped so close I could smell his musty breath on my face. "Tashi. Whatever you've learned from spying, you need to tell me."

I forced a laugh. "The commander is a spoiled aristocrat. The only things he cares about are food and his horses."

"I can tell there's something you're not saying."

I pushed past him and made for the door again. "It's nothing. I'll find Pharo."

He rubbed his temples in resignation. "Do you need me to sit watch while you connect?"

"Xi— The commander won't be back for hours. I won't be interrupted." I needed perfect silence, with nothing to break my concentration. Not when the stakes were this important. I imagined Pharo curled beneath a rotting log, at peace as he wandered the forests in another's body. Then I saw Chen's face leering behind him. If she caught an elusive inhabitor in a trance with metal suspended all around him, would she skin Pharo too?

Thinking about my best friend's skin, draped amongst the tracker's pelts, brought the bile up from my stomach. I stumbled to the pot and retched into it while Ugyen shook his head in disgust.

"You are such a weakling. Always crying, vomiting, slinking around," he said, closing his eyes. "Why on earth would a gold tiger choose you?"

KATALA LOOKED down from the upper branches of a sequoia pine. Her paws dangled in the open air. The tree was taller than the highest point of the Dzong's clock tower. Instinctively, I flexed her claws into the bark as my mind settled into the change of body. She made a groaning noise in the back of her throat, but at least I felt anchored, safe, concealed behind a smoke of pine needles.

Pharo knew how to hide. In our early days at the academy, Mistress Lhamo would take us into the woods to play games that rewarded the last to be found. For children used to studying and meditating twelve hours a day, those games seemed a rare taste of normalcy. It wasn't until we were older that we started to understand even those simple pleasures we'd been allowed weren't games at all. Long after the rest of us gave up from cold, hunger, and boredom, Pharo used to stay out all night. I still remember Mistress Lhamo sitting proudly behind her elephant's ears, calling his name, and the great creature lifting Pharo down from a tree, a whole day and a night after the game began.

Katala poked her nose out of the pine needles and sniffed. The scent carried by the wind was human, but it was deeper, muskier than Pharo's and aged like a liquor, partially masked by a haze of other smells: deer, bears, leopards. Our claws dug into the branch. Katala was excited, animated and ready. As always, she sensed what had to be done, and the challenge of the hunt made her happy. The only thing I felt was fear.

She started to climb down the tree, shutting me out and taking full control of her own limbs. I steadied my breathing, pulling on the connection like reins with every bit of strength I possessed. We learned how to force control at the academy, but I'd never tried it before. Katala stopped short, suspended almost vertically on the trunk of the tree. I half expected her to ignore me. She was confused; I felt it through our bond. I always let her manage the hunt, tagging along like a flea in her fur when she went after mountain goat or a takin. Her legs trembled, and pain shot up her claws from the effort of holding her body weight still.

Chen's scent got stronger below us. I needed to do this. Things were different now, and our hunts in the woods weren't a game like they had been at the academy. Pharo was out in this forest somewhere, and he was the only person left who meant something to me. If I let Katala handle this too—if I didn't protect him—I'd be a coward forever.

Katala sighed. Then I felt her consciousness shut down and drift off into a dreamlike state. Her lithe body, teeth, and bladelike claws became my weapons. It wasn't surrender or submission; it was pure trust. Her trust almost killed my resolve. For the first time, I felt responsible for her. I licked my lips and sniffed the air, trying to feel some ownership of this body I had occupied for so long but never controlled.

I climbed down the tree one step at a time, ignoring the screaming pain pulsing up through my claws. I heard Chen's footfalls now, her lumbering, heavy gait as she crunched over frozen leaves. Stopping at the lowest rung of the canopy, I rested on a branch, still fifteen feet in the air, and waited.

I couldn't let myself think about the sweet bread she'd given me or the way she'd offered to take the blame if I was caught stealing. I didn't know what kind of person the tracker was beneath the stink of the carcasses she wore. I only knew that if I didn't do this, Pharo might die.

Chen walked below me. Her bow was out, but she held it loosely, and it swung with her arm as she walked. I held my breath. A white snow hare nibbled a blade of tall grass, pressed up against the roots of another tree. Chen whipped sideways, pivoting and nocking an arrow so fast it blurred into a single movement. She pulled the bowstring back and let the arrow fly.

I pounced and extended my claws midair. Chen looked over her shoulder, turning as I landed, trying to angle the bow and nock another arrow. But then my weight was on her. My claws ripped through her fragile skin like a warm knife in frozen cream. I tore at her throat with Katala's sharp teeth. The snap of bone, a low whimper, and then her chest folded in on itself. She gurgled blood.

CHAPTER 7

IT WAS nearly midmorning by the time Xian came back, and rays of purple sunlight filtered through the window. He slammed the door behind him, steps heavy. I huddled under my blanket, squeezed my eyes shut and pretended to sleep.

The guilt I'd expected after killing Chen never came. I'd thought her spirit might haunt me instead of starting the long journey back to Myeik and its resting place. I could almost hear her making promises to hunt me in the afterlife and smell the ghost scents of her furs. Instead, my sleep felt fuller, deeper than it had in weeks. I'd done what I had to, and the gods rewarded me with temporary peace.

Xian tossed his pack onto the bed and fell backward onto his mattress. "I know you're awake."

Cautiously, I opened one eye. He stared at the ceiling, making no move to take off his furs or boots. I propped myself up on my elbow. "Should I help you with your clothes? Bring some tea?"

Xian shook his head, running his fingers wistfully over the cashmere blanket. He lifted it and pressed it to his cheek. "Chen didn't return last night. I have to ride out again with another party."

I looked down and bit my lip, not out of nerves, but to make sure the smile of pride rising from inside my chest didn't show on my face. What was wrong with me? Was I happy about being a murderer? I hadn't hated Chen, not really, but Pharo was safe now and would live until all the teeth dropped from Faern's mouth. Or at least until the next time he decided to do something stupid. "Just one night? I don't think that is cause for concern... not yet, anyway...."

"No. Since she hunts alone, she has orders to check in every six hours. She wouldn't stay out so long." He shivered with exhaustion, buried his face in the blanket, and moaned.

"Maybe she got lost? She doesn't know this area, after all."

He barked a laugh. "She's a tracker, Tashi. Trackers don't get lost going for a walk in the woods."

He rolled over and looked into my face. The intensity in his aquamarine stare forced my concealed smile to reveal itself. He raised a brow, and a deep laugh made wrinkles at the corners of his eyes.

All my thoughts of manipulating him vanished. As his gaze traveled downward, my body betrayed me. I felt heat rise from my chest to warm my cheeks. I'd killed one of his people, and I felt no remorse. He was my enemy, and yet I just wanted him to look at me like that forever, in a way no one else ever had before, with desire.

Xian groaned and sat up, shattering the dream. "You're to work in the camp today. With all the patrols, we're short of men. I need you to clean equipment, because all the infantrymen will be with me. Ordinarily, we wouldn't let a foreigner touch our gear, but circumstances force it until we get more men from the south. The stewards will show you how."

"You're not fit to ride out again." A protest formed on the tip of my tongue before I could bite it back.

Xian caught my eye again, then winked. "Is that concern?" Sitting up, he fished under the bed for a spare tunic and threw it at me. "Get dressed. The regiment is expecting me back."

Rubbing the sleep from my face, I caught the tunic and smiled. Today, the square military cut seemed more appealing, more in line with how I felt. I yanked it on. It smelled of earth and woodsmoke, pine needles and horse sweat, made from a fabric so smooth it felt almost like a whisper against my chest. It dangled from my frame, cut for someone much larger... and for a moment, I let myself imagine the feeling of its owner's arms wrapped around me, enveloping me as completely as the scent. I shook the feeling away. Xian was as likely to embed a knife in my chest as hold me close.

Xian reached for the door. A weary grin spread over his face. "If that tracker turns out to be asleep in a tree somewhere, I'll kill her myself."

I nodded, following him through the door and into the brisk winter cold. He wouldn't find the body. Katala would make sure of that.

Zeyar waited for us outside. He leaned against one of the courtyard pillars. He chewed a fresh cherry blossom and spat it like tobacco as we approached. I wondered what Ugyen would say to him if he saw what Zeyar had done to his precious tree. The steward lifted an arm to salute Xian and then took me by the sleeve. "Come on, you. There's work to be done and not enough hands to do it." He bowed to Xian and grimaced, exposing his yellowing teeth. "Happy hunting, Commander."

Xian dipped his head in an almost mocking half bow. Then he took a deep breath and seemed to exhale out the tiredness, forcing himself to stand straighter. I wondered how long he'd been doing that—putting on a show for his men as he ignored his body's rhythms. He strode out the front gates without another glance at me. With my free arm, I pulled the collar of the tunic over my mouth and inhaled him.

Zeyar's grip on my sleeve tightened. "So you've been lying in bed all morning, is that it? While your betters scurry about looking for that pompous messenger. Well, we'll soon put the world to rights. I've three dozen saddles for you to clean."

"I thought you didn't want me to clean saddles," I grumbled and yanked my arm away. "You told me to leave Xian's alone."

He reached out to strike me, but I dodged back. Zeyar stumbled in the snow and cursed. "That was a special case. Don't forget your place and be calling the commander by his given name. I get that he's treating you more like a spoiled pet, but don't forget what you are. A bit of hard work will fix you."

At another time, in another place, he and Ugyen would have been friends.

Zeyar led me out of the courtyard and behind the monastery. Yellow supply tents and makeshift stables for horses stood in neat rows, built over ruined crop fields. Stalks of half-grown wheat lay discarded in piles around the camp. Undeveloped carrots were strewn amongst the tents and dripping from the mouths of sweaty horses. When the army moved on, the monks would be left with nothing to eat but the things they could find in the frozen forest. The image of Ugyen stumbling through the woods with his staff, rooting through leaves to find a handful of scattered berries, cheeks growing ever gaunter, made me feel a twinge of pity for him.

When we reached the first of the stable's rows, Zeyar tugged me into a vacant stall. Sweaty saddles and bits crusted with hard grass lined the edges of the stable. In the center, someone had positioned a stool, a bucket with a sponge, and a small blunt dagger to scrape away the filth.

Zeyar smiled. "I'll be back in an hour. By the time I return, I expect all of these to be spotless." He bent down and tugged a dark red suede saddle toward me. "This is my personal saddle. I will inspect this one first. I hope the monks have taught you something of practical use. Get to work."

He closed the stable door behind him as he left. I heard him fumble with something metal, followed by the unmistakable click of a padlock being fixed into place. He grinned as he locked me inside the cage like an animal. I swallowed as the feeling of being enclosed took over, using all my self-control not to reach and connect with Katala. I'd always felt trapped and uneasy in small spaces.

Trembling, I began undoing the buckles on Zeyar's saddle, separating the leather so I could clean it more thoroughly. His saddle was caked in a thick layer of dust, moistened into mud by sweat and horse spit. The steward had clearly neglected his own tack in favor of other duties. I picked up the dagger and began scraping at the top layer of grime. It stuck to my fingers and got under my nails, coloring them black in seconds.

Sighing, I plunged the girth in the water bucket, hoping to soften the dirt. I'd never actually cleaned a saddle before and wasn't really sure how to go about it. When I pulled it out again, the water in the bucket had turned an ash gray. Liquid mud dripped down the front of the tunic Xian had lent me. Growling to myself,

I bore down with the knife. A delicate pattern of interwoven ferns appeared on the leather's surface. I scratched it away with the blade, peeling the top layer from the leather, and felt the hot glow of victory at having ruined the design.

Just below the buckles, a shallow crack cut across the leather. I picked up the saddle soap again. Zeyar would expect me to massage the fault, work the hide until it softened, even though the girth was stable and would not split. Submerging my arms in the bucket, I worked the soap into lather.

The ice-cold water numbed my fingers and made them stiff and clumsy. The soap slipped into the straw. The knife glimmered next to my foot, and a wicked idea took root inside me. As my heartbeat increased, Katala tried to activate our connection, intrigued by whatever it was that made me both excited and fearful. I gave way and allowed Katala's wordless consciousness to flood my body. She didn't know how to control my movements, but the presence of her, the ruthlessness of her energy, was enough to give me courage.

I picked the knife up and drew the blade across the girth's weakest point. Applying pressure, I whittled and scraped at the cut until only the thinnest layer of leather held the girth together. A sharpened dagger would have severed the leather completely, but in giving me the equivalent of a butter knife, Zeyar made this possible. The girth looked whole at a quick glance, but any sudden movement or stretch and it would burst, the saddle would slip, and the rider would fall to the ground.

I only had to wait until Zeyar tried to gallop.

Katala broke the connection, her interest fading as my heart rate slowed. I hastily finished wiping down the rest of Zeyar's saddle and rested it back against the wall.

There was no way he could prove I'd cut the leather—it was already worn and the saddle was old. At least I hoped he couldn't. I swallowed. Suddenly, too late, I wondered what the penalty might be for intentionally sabotaging what amounted to military gear. As I worked my way through the tack, fear made my insides run colder than the icy water in the bucket. I'd scraped off the girth's pattern; maybe that was enough to condemn me. The old steward might argue I had mutilated his saddle and tried to harm him. In the years Zeyar had ridden with the company, surely others would have seen the fern design. What would he say? Would he notice at all, or would he believe anything that happened was just an accident? Most importantly, what would Xian do about it?

ZEYAR GRUNTED when he opened the door to my makeshift wooden cage. "Still dirty, but they're needed. Let's go. The commander should be back soon. Go wash yourself and get pretty for him."

Seething at the implication, I stumbled out of the stall. But instead of making for Xian's rooms, I ran to the kitchens. I didn't want to be anywhere near Xian if Zeyar found out about the girth. Plus, if Pharo had returned, I was sure I would find him there.

Even with competition from the skewers of meat dripping fat and juices down into the fire, I could still smell him. Pharo's stench dominated the room. His odor hit me as soon as my feet crossed the kitchen threshold. Wolf musk, pungent, gamy, with a wet saltiness like wind coming off the sea.

Pharo sat by the hearth, wrapped in a damp cloak that reeked of it. His shoulders shook, and he hid his face in the crook of his arm. The sight of him openly crying unnerved me. He'd seen me sobbing some dozen times, but I'd never seen him like this.

I couldn't just stand and watch him, so I cleared my throat. He turned toward me with shadows and tears under both eyes and a bruise across his temple. I sank to my knees and edged toward him to wrap my arms around his back. Pharo was the strong one, and it broke me to see him like this.

We leaned on each other and just watched the flames dance for a moment before I asked, "What happened? What were you thinking, going out there like that, with your human form?"

He shrugged and touched the bruise with his fingertip. "This didn't happen to me out there. It happened when I came back."

"Ugyen?"

"He's an abusive little shit. If we weren't trying to blend in here, if he wasn't already injured…." His lip shook, from rage this time, and his hands balled into fists.

I stroked his shoulder. In moments like this, when it seemed okay—friendly—to touch him, I took the opportunity. "He's trying to protect us. I know it doesn't seem like it."

"I couldn't just sit here and do nothing." He grinned suddenly. "I saw Katala."

"I know."

"Oh." His enthusiasm dimmed. "You've been out? Were you looking for me?"

"Ugyen didn't tell you that when he hit you?"

Pharo shook his head. He patted my shoulder, and the grin returned, patronizing this time. "No. I worried you, huh?"

I pushed away from him. "She was after you. I had to look for you."

"Who? That tracker from the south? Pfft. She doesn't worry me. She's used to tracking normal animals. She'll never catch us. What do they have in Myeik, anyway? Goats, fish?" He laughed. "Nothing to build a tracker's skills."

"She killed a snow leopard, Pharo." Anger made my cheeks burn. "What was I supposed to do? Faern is slow. He's old. He's not invisible like he used to be. He limps, he stumbles. Stop kidding yourself."

"We trained for this, Tashi. For years. I'm not going to get caught by some Myeik idiot."

"No, you won't." I crossed my arms over my chest. "I took care of it."

"You took care of it?" he repeated, stroking the stubble around his chin. "What is that supposed to mean?"

I met his gaze, pride and steely residual anger welling inside me. "You know what I mean."

His eyes widened. "You… you killed her? Katala killed her?"

"Shh. Don't say it so loud."

With a loud whoop, he clapped my shoulder hard. "I knew you had this in you. See, you'll be fine. Even when I'm gone. You can do this."

"I don't want you to go anywhere, Pharo." My voice dropped to a whisper.

"I only came back to tell you I was going." He shifted, squirmed, and his eyes traveled to the floor. "I found them… well, they found me. The rebel camp is closer, and they're moving farther south all the time. I can't do anything from here, but if I go to them, I can be useful. Even slow and part blind. I can take messages and things. And Faern can live with me at night, inside, so that might make things a bit easier. He won't have to struggle quite so much anymore, and I can feed him. Master Amo is there, from the academy. He's organizing things."

"You came back to get me?" Hope and fear squeezed my heart so tightly I felt unable to breathe.

Pharo didn't meet my eyes. "You have to stay here. You're too well-placed."

"So you came to say goodbye?" My voice came out as a squeak.

"And thank you. And not goodbye, just… see you later, I guess. I'd take you with me if I could. But everyone agrees… Ugyen, Master Amo… you have to stay. We might not get a chance like you have again."

I could tell from the way he fidgeted with the hem of his red robes that he hated himself for leaving me.

A sob blocked my throat. I couldn't tell him that I might have ruined all of it if Zeyar managed to convince Xian of my guilt. All because of a cruel steward and a stupid prank. Pharo closed the gap between us. I leaned into his chest and inhaled a desperate last breath of him, the wolf-scent made sweet by grief. I was lucky, wasn't I? To have had real friendship at all? Even if I'd never get the chance to experience something more. He pulled me close, and my head rested under his chin. His arms were strong, but they trembled.

WHEN I returned to Xian's rooms, vision still overbright with tears, Zeyar waited for me. He sat in the foyer with another, huskier man I didn't recognize, sipping chai masala from a porcelain cup. He smiled when I entered, while the other man scowled.

"This is the one," Zeyar said. I suddenly noticed the layer of mud caked on his side. My stomach dropped. He spoke quickly in Myeik. "They're the commander's pet, but that shouldn't matter. They endangered me and probably meant worse."

The officer sighed. "You don't have proof of that."

Zeyar squinted at me. "You can tell by the look in their eye. They resent us all. Doesn't fear us as they should. The commander can find another pretty monk to warm his bed—plenty around in a place like this."

The other man took a deep breath and held up his hand for silence. He looked repulsed by what Zeyar suggested. Looking at me and switching to Thim, he asked, "I will ask you this once, and look at me when you answer. Did you cut the girth on this man's saddle?"

"No," I said, trying to keep my tone forceful but not defensive. "Of course I didn't."

"Liar," Zeyar spat. "Sir, they're lying. I know that my girth was a bit frayed maybe, but never enough to split. And the pattern? It was cut clean away. A bit of mud never did that to leather."

"What do you say to that?" the other man prompted.

"I just cleaned. That's all. His saddle was in rotten condition."

"Make them talk. See if they says the same when we take them below." Zeyar sprang up from his chair. "All these Thim, these monks in particular—they're sneaky, they're cheats. They conceal those cursed wizards and work with them. I've never seen anyone fight like the wizards do, sitting at home drinking tea while using their powers to make the very animals in the forest turn against us. I told the commander not to take one for his pet, and look what the coward's done."

"You forget yourself, Zeyar." The other soldier rose as well and placed a restraining hand on the steward's arm. He lowered his voice and switched back to his own language. "They may be guilty, but torture the commander's servant while he rides out? Have you lost your mind? Do you know what Xian would do to *you* if he found out you instigated something like that?"

"He'd see reason… he'd know I'm right."

The officer shook his head. "The commander's a boy… but there's something unnatural in him. He's like his father. Like all the Wunna family. I know that Thim wizard killed your mistress, but your grief makes you unstable. The commander would have the skin whipped from my back just for listening to you, if he found out."

I trembled. The soldier's words rang in my ears. *Something unnatural in him. Like his father.* And now my fate depended on Xian.

"So you're just going to ignore what they've done?" The steward ground his teeth. I stepped back out of reach of his yellow claws.

"No," the officer said. He released Zeyar's arm and took my bicep instead. "We'll put them in a holding cell so they can't run, but there's no sense pressing them here. Until then, try to relax. No sense giving yourself a heart attack over a little mud. If they've done it, they'll hang. Xian's a bit rash, sure, but he'd not keep a pet bent on killing us."

Zeyar folded his arms over his chest.

"We wait on the commander," the officer barked. "That's final."

CHAPTER 8

THEY DRAGGED me to a cell deep in the monastery catacombs. Frozen cobwebs hung from the dank ceilings, and the wind whispered through the twisted hallways. As we marched down the cellblock, the wind's sounds grew louder, and I could have sworn I heard someone howling. Zeyar flung me inside a cell at the end of the row with relish. I was too paralyzed with fear to fight back. The officer simply stepped aside, pressing his sleeve to his nose. I landed in a puddle of something that felt like water but smelled of rot and acid, like a clementine left in the sun too long. Then the steward slammed the thick door and left me in total darkness.

When the door sealed, terror washed over me. I was so deep beneath the earth. I'd never liked small spaces, and the cell was barely long enough for me to lie flat. It stood just paces from the place where Xian had tortured Ugyen, and the specter of his screams seemed to linger in the air.

I pulled my fur tighter around my body. I tried to breathe in the slow rhythm we'd learned at the academy for meditation. If the legends were true, the half souls of the inhabitors I had known waited here in the catacombs, so I wasn't alone. I imagined Mistress Lhamo, sitting cross-legged beside me, her withered hands folded over her knees. Her elephant had died a stone's throw from the monastery gates, so her human soul would look for him here. I imagined her diminutive, bedraggled form stumbling up the mountainside with a gnarled walking stick and an old waterskin. For some reason, I pictured her soul as her body had been: weathered, but tough and determined. Who knew how far the other half of her soul would have to travel to reunite and set her free. If I died here, at least Katala was close by. I wouldn't linger in this dark purgatory very long.

We hung rows of colored flags from the cliffs and trees, leading to the monasteries from all the villages. You could see the fluttering rainbows suspended beneath bridges and stretched across ravines all over Thim. We believed that once the soul left the body it needed the flags to lead it to the afterlife. For inhabitors, the flags led us to the catacombs where our souls could reunite with those of our bondmates.

I pressed my head against the wall. I could almost feel Kalx's warm presence and picture the smile twitching at the corners of his once-mischievous lips. It was comforting to imagine that would stay with me until the Myeik strung me up. My soul could reside with them afterward, until Katala took her last breath.

I didn't dare try to reach for her. Not when Zeyar could come back at any moment. Not even to say goodbye.

"Hello?" a voice croaked in the darkness.

Startled out of the daydream, I looked around for the source of the noise.

"Hello?" the voice repeated, louder this time, seeping through the walls behind me.

I pressed my lips to a crack in the stone, whispering, "Hello? Who are you?"

The voice responded, gasping through a fit of watery coughs. "Abbot Thale. And you?"

Anger knotted in my stomach. The monks were nothing to me, but when I'd seen the abbot he'd looked close to death already. While this old man lay cramped and half-frozen in a wet dungeon, Xian slept in his feathered bed beneath sumptuous mink and bear furs.

"Tashi… the one Ugyen was supervising." I didn't know if he'd remember my name, but in case Zeyar was listening outside, I didn't want to give too much away.

"Ahh," said the abbot. He started to cough again. His tone was light, but I heard the accusation in his gentle words. "You haven't been careful."

"No," I whispered.

"Is it fixable?"

"Maybe."

"We're all counting on you."

Shame made me study my feet. I could almost feel his disappointment through the wall. I had to fix this. Somehow, I would convince Xian to give me another chance.

A BEAM of dull light filtered into the cell. I looked up to find the door open and Xian standing there, holding a torch and just watching me. He was covered in mud, still wearing his yellow travel cloak and riding boots. I looked around him for Zeyar and the other officer.

Xian sighed and closed the cell door behind him. "So is it true? Did you do it?"

I pulled my knees up to my chest and didn't say anything.

"I can't help you if you lie to me." He sat on the ground beside me, wrinkling his nose at the smell and wetness. Then he grinned, though he still watched me with eyes like granite. "Well, I could if I wanted, but I won't help you unless you're honest with me. I have to trust you if you're going to stay with me. Did you cut Zeyar's girth like he says?"

My heart started beating like a deer's when Katala had it cornered. What should I tell him? If I told the truth, I could hang for it. But if I lied, and he knew it, the outcome would be certain. Would he know? Those aquamarine eyes bored through my forehead, as if he could read my thoughts.

"I...." I couldn't even take a breath. Heavy fear crushed my ribs. "Yes."

For a full minute, Xian said nothing. I just listened to the two of us breathing. My own breath came in faster and faster gasps, and his slow, steady, too calm. His peacefulness unnerved me.

"Why?" he asked. "Remember—the truth."

What was the truth? Had I done it for the cause? Or had I done it out of spite—out of pure resentment for Zeyar and the way he treated me? The way Xian's eyes seared into me now was worse than any headache from Katala. I licked my lips.

"He… he… torments me." It sounded dramatic even to my ears.

Xian laughed, but I didn't dare relax. "He's a miserable old cunt." He rested his hand on my shoulder. "So it was all about Zeyar, then? Him personally, and nothing else?"

I traced a crack in the floor with my finger. A flush of shame from the lie I'd told crept up my neck. "What else would it be about? I just wanted to make him fall… not to really hurt him… just embarrass him. To get him back."

Xian slipped his hand into mine. It was rough and damp with sweat, but my fingers closed around his and squeezed anyway. It was nice, sitting here with him like that—like two friends sharing a secret. Or something else I didn't dare think about.

"Well, we'd better go upstairs and rest," he said. "Tomorrow is another patrol. There is a village half a day's ride from here. If there was a storm or she was injured, Chen may have taken refuge there."

"I… I'm free to go?"

"Accompanying me, of course."

"Of c-course," I stuttered. As a prisoner, then. Even more a captive than before. So much for the illusion of friendship.

The abbot coughed again.

"How can you keep him down here?" I asked. I squeezed his palm plaintively. "He's old and sick."

"It keeps the monks under control."

"Under control? They're unarmed men—mostly young boys—with no weapons or fighting experience. What could they possibly do to an army?"

Xian shrugged. "There are many things you can do to an army that don't involve weapons or combat. This ensures Master Ugyen does not pursue those ideas." His hand dropped from mine, and he petted my hair. "No more questions. You'll come with me tomorrow—to the village. One of the monks said the dialect up here can be hard to understand, even for them sometimes. I will need you to help translate what they say."

"I thought you had a camp translator to go on patrols?"

Xian nodded and then tilted my chin up so I had to look at him. "We do. But he will tell everyone what they say. You will tell only me."

ALTHOUGH I'D ridden a horse a handful of times for city functions and pilgrimages, my experience in no way prepared me to counterbalance a horse the size of an elephant as it bolted down a stony mountainside. When they rode into towns and cities, the Myeik liked to make an impression. Xian had lifted his fist in the air, and the soldiers behind us shouted, and suddenly my horse took hold of his bit and charged. I held on to my reins like a lifeline, gripping hard with my knees. The speed and the jarring bounce of the gelding's stride nearly threw me over the edge of the cliff. It would be darkly ironic, I thought without a lot of humor, to be spared a military tribunal, only to die on the back of a horse, riding in one of the saddles I'd cleaned.

The town at the mountain's base was more like a collection of scattered farms and fields than a village. Terraced rice fields framed the town, built into the rising mountain like steps for giants. Melting snow flowed down the terraces in waterfalls, collected in a central pond. A group of farmers squinted up at us as we approached, our horses half-hidden by a cloud of dust and frost-covered leaves. Then, as the glare reflecting off the soldiers' armor faded, farmers dropped their rakes and buckets and fled toward the houses dotted amongst the grazing meadows.

The ground leveled out, and Xian pulled his horse back to a trot at the head of the column. My horse slowed as the herd around him relaxed their pace. I peeled my stiff fingers off the reins and flexed them. An outline of the leather was imprinted into my palms from my desperate grip. My horse let out a deep, wheezy breath that sounded almost like a sigh.

Xian held up his fist again, and I grabbed the horse's mane, preparing myself to be whipped from side to side like an egg in a bowl. But instead of speeding up, the column halted. I tried to relax again, but the unspoken system of communication unnerved me. I didn't have a clue what to expect next. Throughout the ride, Xian had given dozens of commands through his raised hand. I wondered how many signals they had and how much they could say to one another in a way I wouldn't even notice.

Xian turned his horse to face the men. "Round them up. There's a bigger house in the center. It's probably the meetinghouse. We can use that as a central location. We need to speak to them all at the same time, so don't say anything about what we're looking for."

The men murmured their assent and began breaking up into smaller groups.

A few of them wheeled their horses away, and Xian called after them, "Don't be too rough. When they're too scared, peasants won't have the nerve to speak to us. They're a bit like sheep—it'll be all bleating and huddling together. And we've no actual evidence they're involved with the rebels or will know anything about Chen. But don't be too gentle either. We don't want them thinking they can lie to us."

My horse grew restless, shifting his weight around and whinnying as his companions moved away. When the man immediately to my left joined a group, the horse shook his head and pivoted. Both his front feet lifted off the ground. I bit back a scream.

Xian rode alongside me, took hold of the beast's reins, and tugged sharply. "You're letting him run away with you. You need to check him or you'll end up rolling down the mountain and land in the mud with a broken neck." He studied my position. "Still, you ride better than I thought a monk would. Zeyar thought I should tie you to the saddle before we set off. But I can see that you've done this before."

I hesitated. He'd doubt me if I made my lie too obvious. After the conversation we'd had in the cells, I couldn't afford his suspicion. I nodded. "A few times. When I was a child."

"With your family?"

"No, we used to get a lot of pilgrims at the monastery. When I was a small child, sometimes the visitors would let me ride. They let most of us." I had experience with one half of that lie, at least.

I remembered accompanying Mistress Lhamo to another monastery in the south. She had business to conduct, and since I'd missed the fall blessing, she'd brought me and Pharo along for company. The novices had been fascinated with us—as much with the horses we rode, the clothes we wore, and our soft city accents as with our abilities as inhabitors. A few of the younger boys had climbed onto my horse, whooping and shouting. In her wisdom, Mistress Lhamo had chosen an old gelding for me. The solid old gray barely flinched at the noise or extra weight. In contrast to the sweet dappled gelding that had looked after me throughout that journey, the beast I rode now was a dragon.

A breath of wind swept leaves around us in a spiral. There was something familiar about the feel of the air and the smell of rice fields, lotus fibers, and goats the wind carried with it. I blinked back the sting of emotion, digging my fingernails into my palm.

Three soldiers reached the closest peasant house. After dismounting and tossing their reins to the ground, they knocked the door down and dragged two struggling women outside. A toddler ran after them and screamed with his arms outstretched. One of the men stepped forward and scooped him up, then tossed him over one shoulder like a sack of equipment.

Xian looked away from the scene and turned to me with a forced smile. He leaned over in his saddle and stroked my horse's chestnut neck. "I need a cup of tea. We'll go straight to the meetinghouse." Wrinkling his nose in disgust, he added, "I brought my own tea leaves. Who knows how these people live like this. They should have water we can boil. Or at least some snow they can melt."

"I'm from a place like this," I said. If I had dared to release my reins, I would have crossed my arms. "They'd have tea leaves. Some of the best in the country gets grown in villages like here."

Xian just snorted.

"Have you ever even tried tsheringma? It's the best."

Xian stared down at my horse's withers and pressed his lips together. "We'll try that, then."

I wished I hadn't said anything.

He nudged his mount forward. The dragon-horse jerked his head again and followed his friend with no instruction from me. We trotted down the hill as the soldiers continued to burst through doors and pull people from their wooden cottages. The house at the center of the town stood two stories high, built of red brick and cemented with dark mud. Smoke rose from a hole in the pine-thatched roof, smelling of wintergreen and pig fat. Xian grimaced and wrapped a section of his cloak over his mouth and nose. To me, the smoke smelled of memories.

As we approached the biggest house, an old man scrambled out to greet us. He left the door ajar, and the smoke poured into his muddy yard. His back was crooked, and he had marks on his cheeks that looked like bird tracks across wet sand. Raising both arms, he waved his hands at us to show they were empty. Xian motioned him closer.

Stumbling, the man waded through the ankle-deep mud toward us. Then he lowered himself onto a rotting stump. He squinted up at us, but it was me, not the commander in his shining gold-leaf armor and yellow cloak, who caught the old man's eye. Brows raised, he pointed at me with the end of his stick and spoke our language in the thick mountain dialect I'd almost forgotten. "What are you doing here? And with them? You shouldn't be here. Not now. I see what you are."

Xian tapped my shoulder. "He's speaking too fast. I can't understand him with that mountain accent. Make him slow down."

The old man crossed his arms over his chest.

"I'm a translator," I said, speaking clearly so Xian could follow what I said. My heart hammered in my chest. Would this old man reveal me?

The man spat on the ground. If anything, he sped up when he hissed, "You're better than that. Get away from them. Do not help them enslave us."

I swallowed hard.

"What is he saying?" Xian demanded.

"He's telling me I shouldn't be helping you," I said. He claimed not to understand, but after the affair with Zeyar's girth, he could be testing me. Who knew how much of that exchange he'd already understood? I decided to tell a half-truth.

With a growl, Xian pulled his sword from his belt. At first I cringed, thinking he'd caught me in the omission. Then he pressed it into the peasant's chest and whispered, "You'll help us too, if you know what's good for you. We're looking for someone. We need to ask your villagers a few questions. Then we'll be on our way."

I couldn't watch him hurt this defenseless, old man like he'd done to Ugyen.

"Stop," I said. Xian's eyebrows shot up. I laid my hand on his shoulder to soften the command, but his arm twitched at the contact. "They're scared as it is. You don't have to make it worse. Your soldiers are bad enough."

The old man's eyes traveled to the dirt, but a smile twitched at the corners of his lips.

Xian leaned toward me, bringing his lips so close to my ear I felt his breath. I could almost hear him grinding his teeth. "Don't do that. Challenge me in private if you wish, but not in public. And it's not because of my ego. If the army thinks I can't control you, they will make me get rid of you. And worse, they will think I can't control them."

I glanced around. "None of them are here to see."

Xian shrugged. "There is always someone who sees. Tea," he said, speaking to the old man this time. We want tea."

THE TOWNSPEOPLE pressed themselves against the meetinghouse walls, huddling together as far away from the soldiers as they could.

Most of the army waited outside, but a handful of barrel-chested men stood behind the chair and the crude writing desk Xian had dragged in from another house. My captor sat at the wooden table, legs crossed. He inhaled the steam from the tea, casually relishing the fragrance as if he were at a dinner party, then glanced about the room as he drained the cup.

I rested with my back against the wall, needing to relax the muscles in my sore legs. As soon as I'd sat down, the townspeople had scooted away. They practically piled on top of one another to avoid brushing shoulders with me, as if whatever disease it was that made me serve the Myeik might seep in through their skin.

Fear dripped down the walls like rainwater. *Why has the army come here?* the villagers whispered to one another. They had nothing. Nothing to take. No food to feed the soldiers or space for them to camp. *The army needs slaves; that's the only option*, some of the women speculated, mouthing the words to one another so their children couldn't hear. When they noticed me watching them, they pulled their children closer and spoke their concerns behind their hands.

I did my job. I listened to them speak in hushed whispers while Xian surveyed the room that looked like my childhood home with that same look of disgust.

Xian set his cup down on the table. He rose to his feet, and one of the soldiers behind him cleared his throat. The room froze.

"We are looking for one of our trackers," he said, turning to look around the room. "She disappeared two days ago. This woman is valuable to us. If you have any information or have seen a lone soldier come through this town, please speak."

None of the villagers spoke. Some of them turned away and hid their eyes.

Xian looked at me and gestured toward them. "Don't they understand me?"

"I think they do," I said.

"Repeat it. Make sure. Ask the right questions."

"I don't know—"

"Just ask." Xian lowered himself into his seat again. "Make sure they understand."

Pins and needles shot up my calves as I stumbled to my feet. I wrung my hands, surveying the room. It felt strange to have so many eyes on me, when I'd spent so much of my training just learning to blend in. Forty or fifty people clustered in the house, most of them women and children. I wondered how many men the capitol had requisitioned from the village for the infantry and supply teams when the invasion came. It didn't look like many of them had come back. Unlike the Myeik, our infantry didn't accept women.

A child sitting in front of a group of young women caught my eye. The child was small, with dark skin and plump cheeks, chestnut eyes, hair that stuck up at the front, and a crooked tooth that hung over their lower lip. They were like looking into time, a mirror image of me seven or eight years ago. A shock went through my body, and I scanned the room more urgently. But no one else looked familiar, and the woman sitting behind the child with her arms wrapped across their chest was young.

"Have you seen one of them?" I asked, biting the side of my cheek. "She was a large woman. Covered in furs. A tracker, not a soldier."

"A tracker of what?" The old man we'd met in the yard spoke up. He bit off a chunk from a lotus stick and chewed it thoughtfully.

"Of animals." I cleared my throat. "We just need to find her. Then we can return to the monastery and leave you in peace."

"She hasn't been through here." The young woman sitting behind my doppelgänger spoke, drawing my eye back to them. The child felt me looking at them and frowned. Hiding their face under their hands, they moved back into their mother's arms. So they were timid like me as well. A lump formed in my throat, and emotion burned like acid inside me.

The villagers started whispering together again, and I strained to listen, even though I knew they hadn't seen Chen. Xian would want a report of everything they said. Without knowing how much the commander understood of their speech, I needed to memorize everything so I didn't miss something he already knew.

"Maybe something she was chasing got her," the old man said, shrugging. He spoke to Xian, his words slow and clear as he stressed each accented syllable. "Lots of animals out there."

"Not near the monastery," Xian interrupted. "And if it had been an animal, we would have found traces. Bits of her left behind."

A grin of understanding spread over the elder's face, and this time he didn't bother to hide it. He looked right at me when he said, "Animals. Who can say what a wild bear will do? Or how far the tiger will travel? They are unpredictable in their nature and sometimes more human than we imagine."

I cast a sidelong glance at Xian. He stared down at the peasant, mouth quirking into a sneer. But one of his hands reached for the sword at his belt, and I swore his fingers trembled on the hilt.

XIAN DIDN'T speak to me on the ride back.

As we reached the monastery, I started trying to think of ways to break the ice. I could tell he was stressed about Chen, and even more by the villagers' unwillingness to provide any information. I wondered if he was still thinking about the way I had challenged him.

When we stumbled back into the abbot's chambers, covered in snow and melted ice, another messenger sat already waiting. Wrapped in a cloak of white fur, he clutched a letter in his purple fingers. Seeing Xian, his face split with relief. "Thank the gods. I was beginning to fear I'd have to sit up all night. I've been awake long enough as it is."

"Maung!" Xian reached out and clasped the man's forearms before stripping off his own furs and sinking into the chair opposite him. He looked more relaxed than I'd ever seen him. "You've come straight from home?"

I went to sit by the window, far enough from them to give the illusion of some privacy. As far as Xian still knew, I understood nothing of his language. Getting too close would make me look interested.

Maung nodded, stroking the sparse hairs on his cheeks. "A twelve-day ride, since I wanted to avoid the capitol." He held out the letter. "This has not left my person since your father handed it to me. When I arrived at the gates here, the stewards offered to take me to the kitchens and find me a bed, but I was instructed that no one else could touch this, so I didn't dare close my eyes. Not in a wolf den like this."

Xian took the letter and turned it over, examining the blue wax seal. "Is it about my mother?" he asked.

"I don't know, my lord. I only know that it comes from your father. He didn't tell me anything about the content."

"Fine." Xian slipped his dagger into the seal and pulled the letter from the envelope. "Go down to the base. It's behind the left wing of the monastery. The stewards will find you dinner and a place to sleep."

"Shall I return in the morning for your response?"

Xian rubbed his temples. "Yes, and we'll have breakfast here in my suite. You can tell me what is going on at home. The real story. Not whatever bullshit my father has written in this letter. It's really good to see someone familiar, Maung. I don't trust anyone here."

The messenger beamed. Rising on unsteady legs, he pointed toward me. "Destroy it when you've read it so the servant can't look."

"They don't read a word of Myeik."

"If I've learned anything in my time working as a messenger for the court, it's never trust what people tell you, my lord. It's always the ones who pretend to be ignorant that know the most," Maung said.

I schooled my features and tried to look neutral. I couldn't reveal how scared the man made me feel. Maung could spike Xian's suspicions and undo all the progress I'd made in gaining his trust. The messenger obviously knew Xian well enough to feel comfortable speaking his mind. I imagined the commander would pay attention to what he said.

Xian laughed and clapped Maung on the shoulder. But he looked over the man's back at me and caught my eye before I could look away.

Shaking, I rose to my feet. "Do you need something? Some tea brought for your visitor?"

"Maung is leaving so I can read my letter. Go and draw the bath for me."

The messenger raised his shaking arm in a tired salute and left us.

Xian slumped in his chair and stared at the folded paper without opening it. His fingers trembled as they caressed the wax seal. When he caught me looking at him again, he scowled. Pointing to the tub, he snapped, "Didn't I tell you to draw the bath? Get it started. The snow won't gather itself."

The rough edge in his voice had me scrambling for the door in seconds, clutching the water buckets the abbot kept in the corner. I wondered if he was angry with me for contradicting him in the village or for failing to learn anything meaningful at all.

In my rush to the door, I forgot to wrap myself in a fur. The ice-wind seeped into my pores as soon as I stepped outside, like a million tiny needles. I crouched at the edge of the courtyard and began shoveling snow into the buckets with my hands. A burning numbness spread up through my fingers. I packed the snow as tightly as I could, crushing it into solid ice. I didn't want to make another trip if I could help it.

When I entered the room again, Xian didn't even look up. He clutched the open letter in his hands, face unreadable. I hoisted one of the buckets of snow into the tub and suspended the other on the spit above the fire. I waited while he scanned the letter again. I warmed my fingers under my armpits and danced on the spot to make my blood flow again.

Still without speaking, he set the letter aside on the table, stood up, and began stripping off his clothes. His tunic slipped from his copper shoulders, giving me a glimpse of the lithe muscle underneath. I averted my eyes and went to the fireplace to stir the melting snow with the end of a fire-stick.

I turned around again when Xian hissed. He stood ankle-deep in the tub of snow, muscles flexed and rigid against the cold.

"It's not ready yet!" I exclaimed, snatching the second bucket from the fire. "Here, step out. Let me pour this in."

He looked skyward, breathing deeply and biting at his lower lip. He stepped out and moved aside while I poured the steaming liquid into the snow. I knelt beside the tub and forced myself not to turn and look at him even though I could feel the brush of his downy leg against my arm. My fingers tingled as the warm water chased the cold from my hands, but a shiver traveled up my back.

I scooted backward on my knees, folded my legs into the lotus position. I closed my own eyes and willed myself just to breathe in. I had to ignore his presence, the ripples of his back.... I couldn't think these thoughts. I didn't even like him... couldn't like him, after the things I'd seen him do. I heard the water splash as he climbed over me into the tub. Keeping my back to him, I started to get up.

"Stay," he said, and I faced him.

He was submerged up to his navel, chest rising and falling in such an exact rhythm it was like he was trying to meditate as well. He still wore the charm I'd seen in the dungeons, with the small red stone dangling above his collarbone. His left hand hung out of the tub, still holding his letter. The steam made the ink run, and black liquid made a tiny waterfall from his thumb to the floor. Drawing the letter to his chest, he pulled his knees up, allowing his head and back to slip under the water.

As the paper melted to pulp, the ink turned the water as gray as an elephant's skin. Xian didn't surface. I counted to twenty, then a hundred, and still he remained under the water. I knelt up and peered into the tub, wondering if I should pull him up. When we'd had swimming lessons at the academy, Master Thiyn had always said it was impossible for a person to drown himself. One hundred twenty. The grayscale water obscured his form, but I could see his shoulders shaking. How long could he stay down there?

He shot up from the water, gasping. Then his body crumpled in on itself, and he hugged his legs to his stomach. His shoulders continued to shake as dark water dripped down his back. I couldn't see his face, but he kept on quivering. What if he was struggling to get his breath back? After so long under water, had it damaged his wind? I'd lived inland all my life. I knew nothing of drowning. Should I call for help? Reaching out, I grasped his shoulder and pulled him back toward me.

Tears made charcoal rivers that flowed down Xian's cheeks and along the bridge of his elegant nose. He splashed water over his face, rubbing at his eyes. The tears kept falling. With an aggravated growl, he leaned forward and submerged his face again as his back trembled.

I scooted forward and slipped my fingers under his armpits. Then I slowly tugged him upright again. This time he took a deep breath and leaned into my arms. His wet back pressed against my chest. Reflexively, my grip tightened around him. I'd never seen him vulnerable. I'd never imagined him crying.

If Pharo were here, he would tell me to harass him, to play on his sadness and destroy him. But how could I see him as an enemy, someone to be feared, when he was crying? If I took advantage of his weakness now, what kind of monster would that make me? Maybe I could use whatever he would tell me later if he opened up. But even as the thought passed through my mind, bile churned in my stomach. To fight with weapons, physical objects, was one thing. To turn someone's very emotions against them seemed almost too cruel.

"Was it the letter?" I scooped a palmful of water and dripped it through his hair. I had to be careful. He was still himself somewhere, under the ache. And if I pushed too far, I was sure he would snap at me. But there might never be another crack in his perfect veneer, and I had more than enough experience with wild creatures.

"It's my mother," Xian said. "My father wrote to me. Her physician says she's dying—it's the mouth rot—and unless the citrus trees grow again, the apothecary can't make the potion she needs to get better." He peered over at me, water drops hanging from his long lashes. Moisture made his lips look plush and impossibly soft. Then his voice hardened. "Not that my father has gone to see her."

"The citrus trees?" I prompted. I uncorked the little bottle of sandalwood oil that he kept by the tub and began to pour it down his spine. As the scent filled my nose and his back glistened, my body seemed to catch fire. I had never wanted to touch anyone so badly.

Xian sniffled. "We've had a pestilence in the region I live in. Lots of our crops have been failing. My mother.... Well, she has never been strong. That's why I'm here. This land... it has something we need."

My arms slid out from under his. "Something you need? Minerals?"

He shook his head. "Something much more precious and one of a kind. And something the army can't find before I do. If they get it, they'll bring it to our capitol, to the king, and it'll be too far away to help my mother get better. There is a pendant. Like a much larger version of mine. It's hidden here somewhere, maybe even in the foundations of this monastery. It's what gives the wizards here all their power. I need it so our crops will grow again."

Instantly, the image of the note sticking out from his saddle came back to me, as well as Chen's urgent whispers—had I seen anything? What did I know of Xian's peculiar moods? When I was at the academy, we were taught that our power came from the land of Thim itself—our magical kingdom with a life force of its own. Everyone knew that the inhabitors had lived and trained in the academy for centuries and maybe long before the records even began.

"I've never heard about a pendant."

"Oh, it exists," he said with conviction and turned his body around so he could fully face me. "It used to belong to us. My family. A thousand years ago. When we still held the crown."

His body shuddered again, and he slumped forward to put his face in the water.

I tugged him back up, annoyance and a sudden surge of protectiveness making me growl. "Stop doing that. I keep worrying that you'll drown."

Xian raised his sodden head. "I won't drown. I grew up on the lakes. I could swim before I could walk." He sighed. "We're taught not to show our emotions in Myeik. It's part of our culture, to be strong. You must keep things inside or your enemies will exploit you. When I was a boy, I started crying over something—I don't remember what—and my father threw me in the atrium pool. He said that if I had to weep, to do it under the water so no one would ever know the wetness on my face came from tears. I never outgrew that."

His head drooped onto my shoulder, and the shaking stopped. I tightened my hold, wanting but not daring to explore his body with my fingertips. His eyes closed, and I put the bottle of oil down by the pile he'd made of his clothes. The silver dagger stuck out from under a pair of tangled riding breeches. If I had the courage or the will, all I'd have to do to kill a Myeik commander would be to take it and draw the blade across his exposed throat, like he'd done to Kalx. But I needed to know more about the pendant he spoke of. If his information was true, there was a lot I didn't know about the magic that ran through me, that bound me to Katala.

But as I inhaled the scent of him, the urge to use him and find information died. In that moment, with his damp hair brushing against my cheek, I wanted nothing more than to kiss the enemy.

CHAPTER 9

UNABLE TO sleep, I crept from my pallet in the middle of the night, wrapped myself up, and ventured outside while it was still dark. After what I'd seen from Xian in the bath, I was no longer afraid to wander out of the monastery or of raising his suspicion. He'd shown me the most vulnerable side of himself, a side I doubted anyone in the army had ever seen. He trusted me.

I still didn't know what I was going to do with that trust.

I needed to clear my head of all the conflicting feelings I felt for him, and I didn't want to be ambushed crouching in the privy. So I went in search of Katala, reaching for her as I slipped out the monastery's front gate. Letting her consciousness seep into my mind, I tiptoed through the forest in a half trance as she guided me to her den with smells and flashing images.

She met me at the mouth of the cave she'd claimed. The moon made her blonde fur shine silver, her stripes like polished bronze. Approaching me, she rubbed her head against my chest, rumbling and butting me so hard I nearly lost my balance. I began scratching her behind the ears. She dropped to the floor and stretched out on her back.

I knelt and buried my face in her fur. The well-known texture and earthy smell of her brought nostalgic tears to my eyes. I started sobbing into her belly. I hated myself for my weakness, but she was the last familiar thing I had left.

Her friendly trills turned to concern. She started licking the stubble on my head, her raspy tongue scraping my scalp. Logically, I knew she was a killer. I'd seen her kill. I'd even used her body as my weapon… but when we sat like this together and she cared for me like a weak cub, it was hard to imagine my tiger as anything but gentle.

When I'd cried out the last of my tears, I wiped my nose on my sleeve and sat up. Katala blinked slowly and then yawned. I rose to my feet and draped my leg over her back. Opening our connection as she carried my shell of a body into the cave, I tried to clear my thoughts and listen only to hers. In times of stress, it was comforting to get lost in her less anxious mind. She climbed to the back of the den, lay down, and started to doze.

Her belly full of food, Katala slept heavily. She imagined climbing trees with dense leaves, with the sun peeking through onto her coat. In her dreams, she swam and ran, played with her cubs.

I closed my eyes again as our connection broke and my thoughts fled back into my human body. I couldn't let her feel the sudden pain inside me. In her dreams, she was happier than either of us would ever be.

I DIDN'T know how long we slept like that, but when I crawled out through the cave's stalactite teeth, dawn had broken. Praying that no one at the monastery had awoken, I raced back through the forest, nearly slipping on leaves coated by morning frost.

By the time I reached the final clearing, my lungs screamed from the cold air. Sweat glistened and froze on my brow, but I pushed myself into a last sprint. The monastery was still quiet. Maybe I could make it back before even the novices and temple servants stirred. After last night's exhaustion, I doubted Xian would wake before midday. I knew that despite his new trust in me, leaving the monastery had still been a risk. I wanted to avoid making up excuses if I could.

To my left, someone cleared his throat. I whirled around, half expecting to find Xian leaning against a pine, playing with his dagger. Instead, Ugyen sat on a fallen log. He raised an eyebrow without surprise and tapped his cane against the earth as if he had been waiting for me. I stopped, but my body stayed tense, ready to bolt for the monastery gates if he tried to hit me like he'd done to Pharo. I was less afraid of his fists than what Katala might do to him if he hurt me. If my pain woke her and brought her running from the cave, Ugyen's life would be over.

"I saw you sneak out." He stretched and cracked his spine. "You're lucky it's only us that did." He pointed upward, and I followed the line of his arm. The biggest falcon I'd ever seen roosted in the trees above us. The bird preened its magnificent white-and-silver feathers but kept one golden eye fixed on me. Its cobalt beak curved at a sharp angle, like a sickle. "What would the commander think if he knew you'd been sneaking out into the woods in the middle of the night?"

"I was careful," I stammered. "And besides, he trusts me now."

"Two days ago, you were thrown in prison."

"Not by him."

"I repeat, two days ago you were in the dungeon!" Ugyen hoisted himself off the log and grabbed me by the collar. He pulled me so close to his face that I could smell the sour milk on his breath. "Do you really think that the commander pays no attention to the suspicions of his own stewards? Of course he suspects you."

When I lifted my chin so my eyes met his, I saw pity as well as anger in his gaze.

"It hasn't been like that," I protested. My cheeks warmed. I wondered if they all thought what Ugyen did—if everyone at the monastery, from the lowest novice to the officers carrying the Myeik banners, looked at me and pitied me.

Ugyen's breath steamed in the cold air. "Well, thank the gods for that. You've a hard enough task as it is. But why risk this?"

"I needed some air. Needed to process some things he's said."

"What things?"

I scuffed my toe along the ground, squirming as his grip on my chin got tighter. Then a surge of anger burst through me. What right did he have to question me like this? When I was the one doing the work and taking the biggest risk? When I was the one close to the commander?

I tried to pull away from him, but he just dug his fingers in deeper. "What are you doing here? Following me? I'm doing my job. I'm staying close to him."

He sighed. "I've been coming out at night, looking for Pharo. He's not listening well at the camp. He keeps sending his wolf down to watch the armies, even though he has been told to let others who are swifter and less obvious go instead. Faern has been seen."

"You know about Pharo's orders?" Were the monks communicating with the rebels? I clung to a fragile strand of hope. If Ugyen had made contact with the rebels, maybe he could take messages from me to Master Amo. My old teacher would have answers. He would know if the pendant Xian sought was real or just a Myeik fairy tale. And maybe I wouldn't have to be alone with everything I was learning. Any kind of contact with my past would be a relief.

Ugyen released my chin and held his arm up. The falcon delicately pulled one last stray white feather. Then she spread her wings and alighted on Ugyen's outstretched arm. She kept her razor talons so carefully retracted that she could perch on his bare skin without breaking it. Her eyes narrowed at me, but when the old monk smoothed his hand over her sleek feathers, she nipped his ear playfully and preened a pine needle from his robes. When he looked at her, Ugyen's hard expression softened into something like affection.

"I've been stationed here a long time. Waiting, protecting this place," he said. "I didn't want to tell either of you about me at first. I thought the less you knew, the safer you would be until you learned to hide what you are. There are things I have to teach you, but you're so close to the enemy… a little slip is easy. I couldn't risk it until I was sure you could blend in."

I looked from him to the falcon as the things I was seeing started to come together. "You're an inhabitor, aren't you?"

"Yes."

My voice shook with nervous energy. "And why are you protecting this place? An old monastery?"

The falcon nipped Ugyen's ear again, harder this time, and a trickle of blood dripped from the lobe. It was as if the bird was cautioning him against giving too much away. I wondered if she went to sleep when they connected or if she stubbornly ruled her own body as Katala did. Ugyen closed his eyes for a second, body going still as the two engaged in silent conversation. When he opened his eyes a moment later, metal hailstones fell all around him.

"We're vessels. All of us. For something much bigger than ourselves." Ugyen raised his crimson sleeve and wiped the blood away. "This monastery is the most ancient building in Thim. When the Myeik first invaded, we were sure they all came just for slaves and our crops. But why are they here? In this monastery? I've spoken with Xian's officers and listened to them grumble. They could have chosen any of the monasteries within a quarter day's ride of Jakar for the hospital. Here we are remote, difficult to reach. The trip up with wounded men is dangerous for all of them. Why should he choose here? Unless he knows that we've kept it here for a thousand years."

Frostbite nipped at my soul. A thousand years.

"I've done some research on our commander friend," Ugyen continued. "His family descends from one of the oldest imperial lines in Myeik."

I swallowed. My hands started to shake at my sides. "Kept what? And why weren't we taught any of this at the academy?"

Ugyen closed his eyes again, and I waited for the metal storm. Instead, water leaked from under his lids and crept down his cheeks. "Every ten years, we pick only one to know and keep the secret. The knowledge is a burden, and many would rebel against it."

"And you're choosing me?"

"You were chosen from the moment the golden tiger selected you. Do you know how rare Katala is? Let us all pray that she saw something I don't." He tilted his head back and laughed. "The sun will be up soon. Return to the monster's chambers. Come and see me in the evening. There are things we need to finally discuss. I'll be in the chapel."

"WHERE HAVE you been?" Xian asked, voice still thick with sleep, as I closed the heavy door behind me.

"I was cold. Couldn't sleep," I lied and came to sit beside him on his bed. "So I went to the kitchens for some soup."

He sat up and drew one of his extra furs around my shoulders. "I'll be so ready to move on from this freezing pit of a country. You should have woken me. I could have given you a blanket. I have more furs in my trunks. I'll have the steward bring them later."

I imagined the look on Zeyar's face as he watched me press a mink or an ermine fur to my cheek. I'd pick the most expensive one Xian kept in his trunk and twirl about the chamber with it hung about my shoulders, gloating. For a moment, I allowed myself the vain fantasy of etching my eyeliner back into place, reddening my lips, and showing myself off in the sumptuous clothes. I wondered what Xian would think of me.

"Thank you."

To my surprise, he colored. The blush warmed the icy intensity in his eyes, making the specks of blue brighten. "Thank you. For last night. I don't think I have to ask you to keep your silence. The men… they can't think that I'm weak."

On instinct, I touched his arm. The hairs on the back of my neck stood up at the jolt of energy that passed between us. "I don't think anybody would think that about you."

Before he could respond, I went to stir the logs on the fire. During the night, it had dwindled to a smoky glow, emitting little heat. With my back turned to him, I dared to ask, "Are we going on a patrol today? To look for Chen?"

"The regiment will not like it, but I think we must pronounce the tracker dead." Xian groaned, and the bed creaked as he flopped back on the pillows. "Of course, we must have something to blame. If we give more attention to this notion that the animals are turning on us, the soldiers will only panic. I'll pick someone from the village."

I stopped stirring the embers and turned to stare at him. "Pick someone?"

"Someone has to be named the murderer."

"You'll pick someone innocent? Punish them for a crime they didn't commit?" A sick feeling made me unable to swallow.

"Why not? It'll make the men feel better."

"Because they're people!"

Xian rolled his eyes. "They're peasants. There are always more living in hovels somewhere. Besides, I only need one."

Setting my jaw, I met his gaze. "Do you think I'm less of a person because my family were peasants?"

"You're not a peasant anymore. That's different," he snapped.

"How is it different?" I sat beside him once more, imploring him, because the murderer he chose could be the grandmother, father, cousin of the child who could have been me. "Any of those children could be abandoned at the monastery gates."

He glared at me for a moment and then picked one of his furs from the end of the bed. Wrapping it tightly around his shoulders, he shoved his feet into his boots and made for the door.

"Where are you going?" I demanded, unable to contain my surprise that Xian, the boy-commander I'd seen slit a throat in cold blood, would run away from an argument with me.

"I have orders to give." He wrenched the door open and stepped outside. The freezing wind seemed to seep into my very soul.

"But—"

"I've heard your counsel," Xian barked. His mouth drew into a thin line. "I'm choosing not to heed it. My soldiers come first."

"You mean their opinion of you! Your ego!" I shouted.

He slammed the door behind him. I wrapped my arms around my chest as sobs of guilt shook me. Someone in that village was going to hang or worse. And I was responsible for that because I'd killed Xian's prized tracker. I was supposed to be protecting my own people, using my skills as an inhabitor to help us win the war. Instead, another innocent would die at the hands of the Myeik army.

My own helplessness filled me with rage. A china cup brimming with cold tea rested on the stand beside Xian's bed. I seized it and hurled it across the room. It cracked against the wall, shattering in pieces over his prized saddle. The opulent smell of jasmine filled the air, making my chest constrict with anger. Xian saw himself as another type of being, one who sipped spices from the west and brought porcelain halfway across the world, above the peasants who lived among the fields and mud. I hoped my words would eat at his conscience, but I doubted he'd think about them again. To him, this was no different than slaughtering a goat for a feast day. The peasant was a sacrifice to keep his men satiated and comfortable, appreciative of him.

I thought about what he had said about vulnerability. If he showed any shadow of weakness, he believed his hold over his men would evaporate. In the bath the night before, all I'd wanted was to comfort him, to soothe the sadness of his mother's illness. Now I wondered how much of his desire for the pendant was about curing the disease in Myeik, and how much of it was simply about power.

I couldn't let the pendant fall into the hands of a murderer.

Rising from the bed with a sigh, I crossed the room to pick up the pieces of the shattered cup. I sat cross-legged on the floor and pulled the saddle into my lap. A dusting of blue and gray porcelain shards covered the cantle, and the suede seat was covered in dark wet splotches. Hastily, I brushed the dust away and set to rubbing the stains with my sleeve. I lifted the girth flap, and a damp slip of tan parchment slid to the floor.

I snatched it up. The handwritten script was tight and flourished. The tea drops made the letters fuse together, obscuring some completely. I spread the letter out on the floor and blew on it until the ink started to dry again.

When the pools of dark liquid turned ashy gray, I lifted the page to my face and squinted at the writing. It wasn't the first page. There was no greeting and the tone of it sounded like it had once been part of a much longer letter.

> *It'll be deep in the heart of some ancient place. They won't have dared to move it again, because they bind their power to the land, and to move it would sever that connection.... The pendant must be carried by something living or*

the heartstone dies, but the Thim will bind it to the earth if they can. There are none among them who could cope with such responsibility.

The Liu family are fools. I trust you to succeed for us.
C

I turned the letter over in my hand, hoping to find some other clue written in the margins. Or at least some indication as to who the sender was. But the other side of the parchment was blank. Whatever secrets the rest of the letter had contained had long since been crumbled and tossed away.

The Chirang monastery was the oldest building in Thim. It was built in an era not even the historians could remember, and our white nest in the mountains had housed monks and struggling pilgrims for millennia.

The pendant Xian wanted was here. I felt it in my very bones. Ugyen had said that I was chosen to learn the secret the moment Katala picked me. Why else would Mistress Lhamo choose to send me here? She could have sent Pharo and me directly to the base where the surviving inhabitors and rebels made their camp. Surely she must have known how close the rebels were to Chirang. She could have sent word to Master Amo and had him ride out to meet us. Instead, she sent me to the source of all our power, relying on Ugyen to teach me what I would need to know in order to keep our secrets safe.

I folded the letter again and tucked it back inside Xian's saddle. I was better placed than any of them knew.

CHAPTER 10

XIAN DIDN'T greet me when he stumbled back inside, flanked by Maung. I could smell the wine on them. The two soldiers sank into the chairs by the fire. Xian pulled off his boots and socks, letting the flames lick against his wet toes.

They sat, unmoving and unspeaking, for a minute, before Maung clapped Xian's shoulder. "I should be away, my lord. You have your reply? For your father?"

Xian shook his head. He chewed the corner of his lip. "Tell him that I have read his letter, and I wish he had seen her himself so he could send me a firsthand account of her condition."

Maung raised an eyebrow. "Just that? He won't be happy."

"Let him be unhappy," Xian said with a shrug. From the way he spoke about this father, I doubted he was the mysterious "C" from the letter. Xian pulled his deep mauve furs up to his ears and turned to face the fire again. "That's all. Thank you, Maung."

The messenger rested his hand on Xian's shoulder and squeezed. "The war will be over soon."

Xian gave a small nod but didn't turn to look at Maung. When he spoke again, his voice came out hoarse. "Thank you."

The messenger stepped away from him and headed to the door without sparing me a glance. Xian slumped in his chair, rubbing his eyes. Still, he said nothing to me.

While he'd been out, one of the stewards had delivered a tray of food. I carried it from the desk to the table beside him and set it down so hard some of the tea splashed out of the cup and onto the back of his hand. He hissed under his breath but calmly reached for the cup anyway, still refusing to acknowledge me.

"Aren't you going to say anything?" I demanded.

"About what?" he asked, keeping his tone bored as he inspected a hangnail.

I stared at him, unable to tell if he was behaving like this to upset me or if he really was this relaxed after ordering a man's death. He took another sip of the tea and raised his eyes to meet mine. "Something on your mind?"

I sat opposite him, perching on the edge of the chair. Emotion made my chin tremble. I wanted to scream at him, to yell "murderer" at the top of my lungs so the whole monastery could hear. I wanted to run from the abbot's chambers and leave my mission behind. Instead I thought of the letter and took a shuddering, deep breath. If I didn't see this through, how many more innocent people would be victims of his quest for power?

But it wouldn't do to give in too easily. Xian would expect me to be upset, and any other reaction might make him suspicious.

"You're a murderer," I whispered. I felt better for having said it, even if no one else would hear.

He had the nerve to roll his eyes. "Don't be dramatic, Tashi."

I opened my mouth to respond, ready to berate him with a flood of abuse, but an urgent knock on the door made me swallow the insults. Xian glanced expectantly toward the door. I glowered at him and sat back in my chair in silent rebellion.

Xian sighed and went to answer the knock himself. After struggling with the half-frozen brass bolt, he pulled the door open, wincing at the gust of cold wind that flooded into the chamber.

A tiny old woman stepped inside, dressed in the army's yellow livery. Pinned to her chest was a golden badge that showed a phoenix rising out of a flame. Her eyes were pale blue, so light that they almost seemed colorless. Her skin reminded me of an elephant, the same grayish hue, rough and cracked, folding on itself. Even though she stood only as high as Xian's chest, he regarded her with wide eyes and then swept a bow so low his hair brushed his knees.

"General," he croaked out.

I scrambled out of the chair and fled to the rear of the room.

The woman pushed past him and took a seat in one of the chairs. As far as I knew, the Myeik had only one general stationed in Thim. From the way people at the academy talked about her brutality, I had always imagined General Liu as some kind of monstrous giant who ate babies for breakfast. In another life, the woman who sat in front of me now looked like she could have been Xian's grandmother.

Her hawkish eyes quickly scanned the tray on the table, and her nose wrinkled at the sight of the spilled tea. She snapped her fingers and pointed to the stained white cloth beneath the food. Her thin lips quirked into a stern frown. "This will not do."

I took a hasty step forward, half stumbling in my hurry to fix the tray, before I realized she had spoken in Myeik and was probably addressing Xian.

Thankfully, Xian had already rushed to her side. He scooped the tray off the table and passed it to me with a scowl. "Bring a fresh tray for the general."

I thought about refusing, to show him that our disagreement wasn't over. But General Liu folded her hands in her lap and glanced up at me with her translucent eyes. She expected to be obeyed. If Xian was afraid of her, I couldn't imagine what she might do to a servant who refused to fetch her tea.

But the general shook her head. "Stay for a moment. You're a monk here, no?"

When she spoke my language, she had a flawless Jakar accent. She could have passed for Thim in any debate or market alley. It unnerved me.

"A temple servant." I bit my lip and my knees shook.

"What do you know of the local people here?"

My chin jutted out, and I chanced a glare at Xian. "That they're terrified."

She smiled at me and then slammed her tiny fist onto the table. I cowered backward, but she looked to Xian, eyes boring into him. "When I wrote to you, I told you to hunt for rebels in the area. I've stopped here to rest my horses and bring you some fresh information from the city before we head north. Instead I'm greeted by other interesting news."

"Really?" Xian stammered. He scuffed his foot along the floor. I'd never seen him look so nervous.

"I'm told that you're arranging a show trial. You have more important work to be doing than questioning a group of starving peasants."

My chin lifted. Was it possible that the infamously brutal general would show compassion when Xian had not?

"The men—" he began, but General Liu cut him off.

"Don't. You're a half-decent commander, boy. Most of the time. Despite your father."

Xian flushed, grinding his teeth together. "Thank you, General."

"Do you actually believe one of these peasants might be guilty?"

"Maybe. It's possible. We've searched everywhere for Chen. No one has found a body."

She grunted. "Still, how many days were you planning to spend? Weeding through peasants? Setting up this ridiculous trial and presenting evidence? You have better things to do. Just get the message to them. Send a dozen soldiers you trust and burn the village to the ground."

A sob rose in my throat. I clapped my hand over my lips to stifle it.

Xian bowed again. "Yes, General."

The general heaved herself to her feet, bracing her stooping back. "I'm getting too old for such long rides."

"Won't you stay and take some refreshments? Tashi will fetch them."

She shook her head, then drew the yellow cloak tighter. "I'm anxious to get to my tent. I've a servant of my own who gives wondrous foot massages. I will take my evening meal with you." Winking, she patted his arm and gave his cheek a little pinch. "Don't look so glum. All my commanders need a good telling off every now and again. But I've brought some of that smoked herring you like."

"You're too kind, General." He pulled the dark fur off his back and held it out to her. "The winds are fierce here, and I fear you are not dressed for the weather. Please, take my fur until your steward can unpack your own."

General Liu cackled. "Kissing my ass now, aren't you? Well, a bit of brown-nosing never went amiss…." She took the cape and draped it over her fragile shoulders. It hung down past her bony knees.

Xian's blush deepened. "It's easy to compliment you."

Her laughter rose an octave. Then her face drew in a serious frown. "I almost forgot. We will discuss this more at dinner, but you can instruct your regiment to keep their eyes open. On the ride here, we spotted an old wolf behaving very oddly. It seemed to track us, but we never saw its pack. One of my archers took a shot at it, but it ducked behind a tree as soon as he fired his arrow."

I went to the fire and knelt beside it, trying to distract myself by stirring the logs. Focusing on the flames gave me an excuse to turn my face away so neither of them could notice the emotions playing out. The Myeik's cruelest general had her eye on Pharo. I had saved him from Chen, but General Liu would be guarded at all times and she commanded the entire army. If I went for her, Katala and I would die. No one would protect Pharo then.

"Odd," Xian said. "It knew to dodge."

General Liu nodded. "Exactly. I found it strange as well. Well, I will be off. Send a few men out for a scout. Let me know by courier what you find."

Xian stepped to the door and held it open for her. He braced himself against the cold wind as the general meandered slowly over. Rising on her toes, she planted a soft kiss on his cheek. She lingered in the doorframe, seeming to enjoy the look of pain on Xian's face as the freezing wind beat against his exposed, pale skin.

"See you for dinner," she said, and left.

When he had pressed the door closed firmly behind her, Xian went to his bed and fell backward on it. He stared up at the ceiling while I stared at him. Rolling onto his side, he caught me looking at him. "I was trying to be merciful," he murmured in the same weary, emotion-edged tone I'd heard him use in the bath.

I climbed onto the bed beside him. "Why didn't you say that before?"

He shrugged. "Technically, you're still my enemy. I forgot myself last night. Besides, I knew what I had to do. I knew you wouldn't like it. And I'm not used to explaining myself."

"But why say all that stuff… about the peasants?"

"It's the truth. If you take emotion out of it, there will always be more peasants." Xian rolled over onto his other side, facing away from me. "It's been drilled into me. You do what you have to for the sake of many."

Hesitantly, I reached out and placed my hand on his shoulder. He sounded so exhausted, so beaten. His skin felt like frozen metal. I cleared my throat. "Are you going to do what she says?"

"We all do what she says."

"Can't you lie? Can't you just tell her you did it? She'll be leaving in the morning."

Xian laughed sharply. "Do you know what would happen to me if she ever found out? It's different at home, but as long as we are here, all of us submit to military justice. Her word might as well come from the gods for as long as I am stationed here."

I was on the verge of tears. I thought of the child from the village standing in the middle of a charred rice field, their cheeks drawn with hunger and their eyes hollow. And then there was Pharo. By now the whole Myeik army would know what Faern looked like. By killing Chen, I'd naively thought I'd saved him. Instead, I'd made everything so much worse.

"When we were in the village, I saw a child. They looked just like me, back before I came to the monastery. They could have been me." I lost the battle against the tears. A trail of warmth slithered down my cheek.

To my surprise, Xian lifted a hand to cup my face. "Hey, don't. They could have been you, but they aren't. You don't know any of those people."

I hated him and his cold, emotionless logic. I took a shaky breath. "I need to get some air."

"Okay," he said, voice small and subdued. His eyes searched mine for something, but I pulled away from him. Donning the last fur draped across the bed, I strode outside in search of Ugyen.

UGYEN SAT cross-legged in the rear chapel, in front of the monastery's largest statue of the Ghungza. His head was bowed as if in prayer, but as I approached I saw his eyes were open and his lips didn't form words. His eyes were harder than the god's ruby pupils, and he wore a disgusted frown on his face. I rested my arm against the doorframe, watching in awe as he stood up, lifted the front of his robes, and began to urinate on the statue's polished gold legs.

I cleared my throat. Ugyen jumped, shook himself, and fumbled with his robes. Seeing me, he breathed a sigh. "Good. It's you. I was worried for a moment it might be one of the novices. I'd have a hard time explaining."

Stuttering until I found my voice, I hissed, "W-what are you... why did you do that?"

He shrugged. "I've never had much time for the gods, and I think recent history would suggest they don't have much time for us right now either. These monks pray five times a day to the Ghungza, and he's shown nothing but contempt for them. For all of us. I wanted a little revenge."

"But you're a monk."

Ugyen raised an eyebrow. "I think we've established by now that I am not a monk." He stood and edged away from the puddle on the floor. "Come. Let's go through to the shrine at the back. We won't be overheard. Only the abbot and I have keys."

He prodded a green jewel on the edge of the statue's sandal and a small door opened at the rear of the chapel. Green smoke drifted out from the doorway, curling up into the air like the tendrils of a wispy vine. Ugyen stepped inside, coughing. I followed him in, ducking under the low stoop. The smoke made my eyes run, the smell so overpowering I could taste it in my mouth. Hundreds of candles lined the chamber's walls, each surrounded by a burning pyre of powdered incense. Ugyen shut the door behind me, sealing us inside the chamber.

"I have so much to tell you, I'm not sure where to begin," Ugyen said, sitting down opposite me and curling his legs into the lotus position. Years of pretending to be a monk had conditioned his body, and even at rest, with only me to see him, he still sat like they did. "Under normal circumstances, you'd have been sent to me next year. We would have had years to converse and study together. I'd have had time to help you understand...."

I covered my mouth with my sleeve, trying to filter the air before it reached my lungs. I hated the war, but at least it had spared me years of study with Ugyen. "Tell me about the pendant."

"I didn't tell you it was a pendant."

"Xian's looking for it." I didn't know why, but I felt a stab of guilt at this admission. The pendant was Xian's secret and one he had entrusted to me. I shook my head, trying to clear the thought. Gaining his trust was my mission, and I was succeeding. I should have been proud to tell Ugyen what I'd learned. Instead, I felt almost ashamed for betraying the boy-commander, my enemy.

Ugyen pressed his lips together. "I thought as much. The Myeik know how powerful it is and what it can be used to do."

"It's not the Myeik," I said. "It's just Xian. The rest of them don't know he's looking for it, and he wants to keep it that way."

He smiled then, revealing a mouthful of half-broken teeth. I wondered how many of them had been cracked by Xian's brutal fists. I didn't remember any gaps in his grin when we'd first arrived. "We may still keep it hidden. He won't be able to look in the open. Not if he doesn't want to risk someone else finding it before him. The Myeik are all suspicious of one another. It's a constant struggle for power over there. No stability."

"He said his family used to own it. A thousand years ago."

He ran his fingers through one of the candle's flames. It flickered and cast long shadows against the wall. "It's possible."

"How did we get it?" I asked. "And why is it kept here?"

"You've heard about Master Tanto?"

Of course I had. He was the academy's founder, and his life story was drilled into us from the time we could fold a meditation mat. "Yes. I know that he is supposed to have been the first inhabitor. And that he started the academy. And that he was the one who thought all inhabitors should be born poor children, rather than the city's elite, so that there would be a balance."

Ugyen nodded. "All of that is true. Tanto was a philosopher. He worked in the palace of the Myeik emperor."

I gasped.

"The emperor had the pendant in his possession. It's an ancient object, far older than either Thim or Myeik as we know them today. The Myeik call it a heartstone, and they believe it's part of a god's heart. The emperor used it to command his subjects, to make the earth bear fruit…. But power made him tyrannical. Tanto dreamed of returning to Thim and using the pendant to create a utopia where no one person would command the stone. Its powers would be split among many and bound to the earth. He wanted to bring us into harmony with the animals and with nature. He wanted balance above everything else."

"The Myeik emperor commanded all the power that is in all of the inhabitors?" I asked, thinking back to my time at the academy. There had been a hundred masters or more, countless novices, and that didn't include those who served in the Dzong or those who patrolled our borders and kept us all safe. "How is it possible for one person to command so much energy?"

Ugyen shrugged. "Greed often pushes the limits of what we think is possible."

I shuddered. If Xian had the heartstone pendant, where would his limit be?

"Tanto decided that an inhabitor's power would always be tempered. We share the pendant's power, and we ally ourselves with animals to remind us to respect the land and the power of the creatures that inhabit it. He believed we should not abuse the pendant the way the Myeik have. And his dream succeeded. Our country is green and fertile. People don't go hungry here."

I raised an eyebrow, barking a laugh I didn't feel. "It succeeded? We were invaded. A quarter of our population is dead, another quarter bound for the auction blocks. It didn't protect us."

Ugyen shrugged. "It cannot be all things. That is when greed takes over."

"This connection to the stone. How does it work? And where is it now? I know it's here.... I... I can feel it." I couldn't explain how I had known it was here the second Xian told me, but certainty coursed through my blood.

Ugyen smiled, putting his hand on my shoulder. It was the first friendly gesture I'd ever experienced from him. "Reach for it. Reach for it the same way as you reach for Katala and you'll see."

I looked askance at him, skeptical. "Reach for a stone? It's not alive."

"It is. Try."

I closed my eyes and reached for the unknown. I felt Katala's interest flicker, and she tried to answer my call. I couldn't feel the pull of anything beyond my gold tiger. The pounding in my temples spread. Pain seared through my skull and seeped out the pores in my skin. My whole body burned and froze, as if I lay buried in ice while someone dripped boiling water onto my frozen skin. I tried to open my eyes, but I was lost, trapped somewhere in the abyss between my body and Katala's.

Somewhere in the haze of thundering pain, I heard Ugyen whisper, "You're pushing too hard. You don't command it. Ask."

I wanted to laugh, but my thoughts felt displaced from anything physical, completely disconnected from a throat and unable to make a sound.

Suddenly Katala's senses engulfed me. My eyes focused on the wall of her cave, and I could hear the low growl in her breath.

Inwardly, I sighed. Of course I would fail at locating the pendant. I'd never been good at anything.

"Katala," I whispered through our connection as her growling turned to rumbles. *"You made a mistake. You could have chosen anyone, but I've been letting you down for years. And I'm afraid because I know I'm not strong enough for any of this."*

I tried to disconnect, but something held my consciousness inside her. I moved her paw and flexed her long claws, marveling at the sheer dangerous power of her.

Ask. Ugyen's words rang again.

I looked around the cave in confusion. How was he speaking to me? I could hear him as clearly as the birds twittering in the trees above Katala's cave. But that was impossible. My mind had settled in this body, and I couldn't use both sets of senses at once. Everyone knew that.

Just like they knew about the heartstone. All the limits on our power we'd been conditioned to know no longer seemed real.

"It's part of you too," I thought, and Katala's growl resonated through her body. *"Help me find it? Please?"*

I closed my eyes again, this time acutely aware that another presence followed me into the darkness. The trust between us was absolute. I relaxed, comforted that even here in a space between bodies, I wasn't alone.

Something solid closed around me. Unable to see, I tried to feel out my surroundings, but I couldn't move. Seized by panic, I was about to drop the connection, but then I smelled something. The fragrance was delicate, almost ethereal, and very far away. Cherry blossoms.

I dropped the connection. Metal stones rained around me, but they were different. The stones glimmered in the candlelight. They were gold now rather than the silver I'd come to expect, and at the center, each of them bore a tiny ruby.

I pictured the monastery courtyard, with the cherry tree standing proud at its center. The sacred tree that Ugyen had warned me never to touch, that bloomed even in the dead of winter when ice made crystals in the air.

"It's in the tree," I panted. "In the cherry tree."

"Good." Ugyen clapped slowly. "I'm impressed. It's not often that someone can locate the heartstone on their first try. We spend so long at the academy conditioning you to ignore it, to focus solely on your bond with your animal, that for many the new task goes against everything they know. Now, I'm sure the commander will expect you back. We will meet again soon. But for now, ask me the most pressing of your questions."

"Why do we keep this such a secret?" I asked. I felt drained of energy, but my mind whirled. "Why don't they teach us about this at the academy?"

Ugyen stroked his chin, seeming to ponder his words. "There are some who say that if we told too many of the pendant's location, it would be vulnerable to theft."

I nodded. It made sense. In a millennium of the academy's history, there must have been rogue students who would have tried to steal all of the power for themselves.

"But that isn't all of it." He sighed, rubbing his temples now. I suddenly noticed the dark circles under his eyes, and I wondered how tiring it must have been for him, to have kept these secrets year after year. "To keep Tanto's balance there is a price. We inhabitors know it all too well. We bind ourselves to other living creatures, and in return we gain understanding and abilities we could never hope for in our human forms. But the price of that is our life. Few of us are lucky enough to bond with creatures with lifespans the length of a human. It was decided long ago, at the beginning of it all, that each inhabitor would bond with one creature. So it has always been. But it doesn't have to be so. We could change the fabric of the spells that bind us, and an inhabitor could have many bonds throughout their natural life…."

My eyes widened, and my heart began to race. Many bonds? Instantly, I thought of Faern stumbling through the woods, his toothless mouth struggling to chew a bite of Pharo's dinner. Pharo. A lump of misery and bile worked its way up my throat.

My Pharo, who was bound to a wolf at the end of his life. My strong, beautiful Pharo, the boy who had been my family and my stability, who I tried not to love because such a love could only end in pain and loss. We both knew better. Had known it since the day the finch girl sang her last sad song. But I couldn't help what I still felt sometimes. Everything I felt for Xian was a shadow in comparison. Was Ugyen telling me that Pharo didn't have to die?

"What are you saying?" I gasped as my words caught up with my thoughts. "Are you saying we could live beyond our bond? That there is no need for us to die young?"

Ugyen grimaced, and to my surprise, tears swam in his eyes. "We live a powerful life. We live twice at once, and we have abilities beyond the conception of normal people… but there must be balance, and so our magical lives are short. Determined by nature and out of our control."

"Someone I love is dying."

"Everyone I grew up with is already dead."

"You sacrifice us. We never get a choice. We're never asked if we want to be inhabitors. My parents just left me with you when I was a child. Nobody asked me if giving up my life was a choice I wanted to make!"

Ugyen shook his head. "I know this is a lot to take in. Under normal circumstances, we would work up to this over a course of months. But there just isn't time."

Faern was old and slow. Whether the general's men slew him or he succumbed to his age, the wolf's days were limited. But without that magic tie, Pharo could live for another sixty years. He could grow old and enjoy a fuller life than any of us ever imagined. He could love without fear. I bit my lip. Even if he could never love me in the way I wanted to love him, he would live and I wouldn't be left all alone.

"It's a lot to process," I said.

Ugyen hesitated and then laid his callused hand on my shoulder. "Sleep on it? Speak tomorrow?"

I nodded but said nothing.

He opened the little door, and I gasped as a flood of fresh air poured in. I scrambled through the opening, but Ugyen stayed behind. "Go," he said, giving my back a little shove. "I have thinking of my own to do."

CHAPTER 11

IN THE morning, Xian shook me awake. I turned over groggily and then shot up as the low blast of a hunting horn sounded through the walls.

"Get up," he said impatiently and paced across the room. "That wolf's been spotted, and I can't find my spurs anywhere. My mare's lost a shoe, so I've got no choice but to take the stallion."

Pharo. My stomach clenched, but I forced myself to rub my eyes with faked sleepiness. "Where have you looked?"

"Everywhere!" He stomped his foot on the wooden floor.

Sighing, I pushed back the warm blankets and began lifting strewn clothes off the floor. I made a show of searching behind the furniture, all the while hoping they were lost and the hunt would be postponed.

"Maybe they're under my bed," Xian said, starting to get down on his knees.

"I'll look!" I raced over to the mattress and crouched down. A glint of silver caught my eye, and I lay on my stomach to reach for it.

"I can't find them," I lied as I made a show of rummaging beneath his bed. My left hand closed around the missing silver spurs. I had to delay him just a little bit longer. Using a trick Kalx had taught me long ago, I slipped the spurs up my sleeve and out of sight.

"Come on!" Xian said, glancing urgently between the door and me. "That was the second horn. I have to go."

"I haven't seen them since you came back yesterday. Did you leave them at the stables or with your steward?"

He hopped in place impatiently, rising on his toes. "No, of course not. My boots are here. Why would my spurs be somewhere else? I need them. Fucking stallion notices right away when I don't wear them."

"You could ride someone else's horse?" I offered, then forced myself to laugh even though I didn't feel like it. "Try something a little easier?"

Xian cast me a baleful look. "In the field, everyone knows me by my horses. It's easy to tell a rider at a distance by his mount. It would confuse everyone."

The hunting horn blew again, a low, grating rumble that reminded me of a leopard's growl. The sound reverberated through me, spreading cold fear. *Run, Pharo*, I thought as the sharp metal points from the spurs dug into my forearm. *Run and don't look back.*

Xian moaned, then banged his fists against the closed door. "The general will skin me if she learns I missed catching a rebel because I couldn't find my spurs."

"I don't know what to tell you. Ride another horse."

His jaw set, and he pressed his lips together. "I'm going. I might not be able to control my stallion, but better I fall off trying that than I stay here."

He threw his yellow military cape over his shoulders and pulled the heavy door open.

As soon as the door slammed, I raced to the privy. Pulling the paper screen behind me, I settled on the floor. The smell was even worse than it had been a few days ago. Cleaning the privies, even the one used by their commander, did not seem to be high on the army's priority list. The once pure air around the monastery had started to stink of unwashed soldiers and horses, shit, and rotting meat.

I reached for Katala. Her response was instant. She felt my panic. As soon as the bond was forged, her heart started to race. Hunting was what she was made for; bloodlust made her senses sing. Pressing her belly to the earth, she slunk out of the cave. I concentrated on feeling out her body, getting used to the shape again. Her stomach was weightless, and her muscles tensed at the slightest noise. Her nostrils flared as she sniffed the air. Hunger made her sharp, as deadly as a poisoned arrow. Trying to track down Faern with the army regiment looking for him might be our last hunt, but at least Katala was as ready as she could be.

I knew that I could get caught. Then Katala would die, and I'd suffer a fate worse than death. But when it came to Pharo, nothing was too much of a risk. I had to try.

The hunting horn sounded somewhere below us on the mountainside, followed by the drumming of a hundred hooves. I squinted down at them, and my heart stopped. Faern hid behind a shrub, his tail tucked, and crouched low. His white-and-gray fur glimmered like polished metal. How long before one of the trackers spotted him? He couldn't run or he'd give away his position. All I could hope was that the army passed him and carried on down the mountain.

Xian rode at the head of the column, accompanied by a standard bearer holding his flag. It depicted a black ship coasting over red triangle water. His stallion pranced from side to side, throwing its head up in his face. Then the horse squealed and swung his haunches into the standard bearer's mare.

The gold mare flattened her ears. The stallion nipped her neck. Xian shouted something I couldn't make out, using his reins to smack the horse. The huge beast quieted, subdued, but the mare lunged sideways toward the woods. The standard bearer tried to steady her, I could see him tugging on the reins with his one free hand, but as the mare twisted, he knocked her slender legs with the heavy bronze flagpole.

Frightened by the pain, the horse stumbled forward and tripped. I watched in horror as the steward slid down her neck and landed just feet from Faern's hiding place.

The old wolf didn't move. Sitting up slowly, the steward wiped cold mud from his face and braced his back. Xian jumped off his horse and rushed to him, pulling the stallion behind by the reins. His actions surprised me. I would have expected him to remain safely on his horse and let his men rescue the standard bearer. After helping the steward to his feet, Xian lifted the flag from the dirt. Something he saw through the leaves made him hesitate. Gripping it from the top, he slid the pole into the shrub to part the foliage.

Faern rested his head on the ground, making himself as small as possible. But there was no way to hide his bright white fur.

"Sir!" one of the soldiers called out. "Sir! Please. Get back on your horse. It's not safe."

Xian's whole body froze for a moment. Then his fingers flew to his belt for his sword. I felt paralyzed myself, knowing what he must see through the leaves. Death stared straight at Pharo, but death had a face I knew now—a face I'd longed to touch.

I expected Xian to alert the guards alongside him, but as he took a hesitant step forward, I realized he planned to slay Faern himself. Maybe he felt he had something to prove to General Liu or to his men, or maybe just to himself after his failure to find Chen, but his desire for glory bought me seconds. My frozen body thawed. In a few silent leaps, I descended the cliff. I could feel the adrenaline spiking in Katala's body. Her claws extended, but I forced them back. I didn't want to hurt Xian even though, if it came to it, I knew I would always choose Pharo. Leaping over Faern, I pushed through the bushes and tackled him.

He fell backward onto the hard earth, gasping as Katala's full weight slammed into him. I heard something crack, but I couldn't stop moving. All around me, men shouted and pulled forward, scrambling for arrows. I flew backward into the cover of the shrubs. Faern was already bolting up the steep mountainside. His bright fur made him an easy target, but it didn't matter. The whole army had seen a golden tiger attack their commander, and the archers only had eyes for one target.

A hailstorm of arrows beat the rocks around me, narrowly missing my paw. Katala's lungs screamed as we bounded up the slick rocks, the cold air cutting off her breath as if we were drowning. A red-tipped arrow grazed her flank, but we made it to the top.

Faern lay on his side, panting, with his yellow eyes half-closed into slits. I sank to the ground beside him. His breath was labored, not just short. Fluid bubbled somewhere deep in his wind. Unbidden by me, Katala pressed her head to his chest. His heart beat faintly, too slowly to make sense after the chase.

The old wolf leaned into Katala and shut his eyes as she licked his ears with her rough tongue. Katala was never affectionate like that. Not with anyone but me. She'd known Faern for years but always kept the wolf at a distance. She tolerated him but never fully embraced him as her friend. If she was comforting him now, something was different. She knew something I wasn't ready to accept.

A flood of emotion broke my connection to Katala. A howl of raw emotion rose in my throat, and I didn't care who heard me as I let it out. I smashed my head back against the privy's wall. I'd revealed myself to the whole Myeik army, and it wasn't even going to matter.

Faern was dying. And Pharo would go with him.

Someone pounded on the door. Hastily, I scooped up the silver stones and threw them down the privy once more. Brushing tears away with my sleeve, I stumbled to open the heavy door.

Ugyen stood on the dais, wearing a heavy brown cloak. It was the only time I'd seen him wear anything other than his red monk's robes. His falcon sat on his shoulder. Her golden eyes looked right at me.

Ugyen grabbed my arm. "We don't have a lot of time. You have to go."

"Go where?" I asked as more tears I couldn't stop slid down the bridge of my nose. I couldn't speak to him now. Not when he was the reason this was happening. If it wasn't for the secret he protected, Faern could die and Pharo could go on. My friend could live on and bond again. Anger sent a shiver through me. "Go away. Get away from me."

His grip tightened. "Do you want to have the chance to say goodbye?"

"What?" I gasped.

Ugyen stroked the falcon's sleek feathers. "Pyan has been watching after Pharo for me."

Leaving the door ajar, I ran to the bed and snatched up the thickest of Xian's furs. I threw it over myself and rushed back to the door. Faern was dying. I had known that for months, but if I could snatch a few last moments with Pharo, I would. I pinched my nose to stop the crying. I wouldn't ruin Pharo's last moments with sadness.

A smile played on Ugyen's lips, but his eyes were downcast. "You ready?"

I scanned his appearance again, taking in the heavy furs and realizing he meant to come with me. "Send the bird," I spat. "I'll follow her. But this is your fault."

"Oh, come on, Tashi. The wolf is old. It's my fault it's dying?" he snapped. "Do you hear yourself? You can't blame me for this. It happens to all of us."

"It happens to all of us because you let it!" I shouted. My hands balled into fists. Rage and love for Pharo made me feel braver than I ever had in my own body before. "You're sacrificing us. That's all we are to you, vessels that you can use and toss away."

Ugyen scowled. "That's not fair. The laws of balance also bind me. When Pyan dies, so will I."

I shoved past him.

Ugyen sighed. He raised his arm, and the falcon climbed to his wrist, fluffing her feathers. "We're on the same side."

"I'll try to remember that while I watch my best friend die," I growled as the falcon took flight.

THE FALCON led me to the edge of a stream covered with a thin film of ice. Pharo sat near the water with his back to me. He shivered in the cold. A halo of fragile silver stones hung in the air around him. I knelt on the ground behind him, hugging him around the chest. His whole body shook. I knew that in his mind, he experienced Faern's pain and the fear of death.

I pulled one of the stones from the air, turned, and hurled it at the falcon. "Get out of here," I screamed.

I didn't know if it was the white bird who watched me or if Ugyen spied on us from the trees. Either way, I didn't want the guardian near me while I said goodbye. Pain erupted in my chest and traveled down my quivering arms. The falcon hesitated, but when I aimed another stone, she took flight with a sad shake of her feathered head.

Closing my eyes, I reached for Katala. She and Faern were lying together under a rocky outcrop now. Her mouth tasted faintly of wolf fur, and she was rumbling, with her body pressed tight against the old dog. A daydream passed through our shared consciousness. Katala imagined herself hunting, bringing a rabbit for Faern. I couldn't hold back the emotion, no matter how much I wanted to spare her the physical pain. Her ribs contracted, and the air froze in her lungs.

She head-butted the wolf gently, and when his eyes rolled toward her, she looked up to the sky.

Come back. I willed Pharo to understand.

The wolf nodded his shaggy head.

Our twin rings of silver stones fell to the earth around us. But for once, I didn't think of them as beautiful. Instead the bright metal against the white of the snow-covered earth reminded me of ash. Everything around us was burning.

"Hi," Pharo said as his head fell back against my chest.

"Hi," I managed to squeak before I succumbed to sobs.

"Hey," he said, turning around and pulling me to him so my head rested under his chin. It was so wrong that he was comforting me now, but I couldn't pull away from the strong familiarity of him, from his gamy scent of wolf and smoke. "It's going to be okay."

"How can you say that? You're dying, Pharo. This is it."

He rubbed the back of his head and tried to smile. Then he flexed his bicep. "I feel okay. Perfect shape."

I laughed, sniffing back tears. "You would say that."

"It's the truth. I know Faern's in pain. His heart's failing and it won't be long, but when I'm in this body, I just feel like me."

"You shouldn't have pushed yourself."

He shrugged. "Faern is old. Even if he lived a life curled by my fire at the academy, he might have had six months left at the most. At least this way, I don't feel like I've just been sitting around waiting to die." His eyes glittered, and he gestured back toward the monastery. "I've been stealing their supplies. I'm not strong enough to go after them directly like you and Katala, but I've been doing what I can."

"Master Amo told you not to," I choked out. I didn't mean to scold him, not now, but it was second nature. All my life I'd been trailing after Pharo, worshipping him from the periphery while he forged on, missing him when he pushed too far.

"I know." Pharo sighed and ran his hand over my hair. "And I'm sorry. I would have stayed with you if I could. I know what they want you to do."

I pushed away from him and looked him in the eye. "No, you don't. Nobody does. They need too much from me. I can't do it."

His tone turned serious. "You have to. You have to keep watch on the commander. It's the closest position we have. The rebels are struggling. We just don't have the numbers, and already the Myeik have started shipping people out of Jakar. They're taking all the strong men, the ones who can still work."

"That's not everything the rebels need from me. If they only needed me to watch—"

"Whatever it is, you have to do it," he said.

"Katala made a mistake when she chose me. Sometimes I think even she knows that."

His eyes closed, and for a moment, fear made my heart stop beating. It would be peaceful when he slipped into the coma, since the decay was happening in Faern's body, not his. I knew that, but I wasn't ready. Then he leaned forward and pressed his lips to mine.

The kiss was so unexpected I tried to jerk my head back. But Pharo's fingers gently cupped my face. The stubble framing his jaw rubbed against my cheeks. His tongue sought out mine with a kind of desperation.

He pulled back slowly, nibbling my bottom lip.

I looked at him questioningly. "You don't... I thought...."

"I wanted to."

"Since when?" I asked, and I was glad the tears were already falling so he might not notice the trembling in my voice. I didn't ask whether he'd wanted to kiss *me* or if he'd just wanted to experience the kiss itself. I couldn't, not when whatever he said now could be the last thing he ever said.

"I have for a long time," he said and squeezed my shaking hand. "Even though I knew I shouldn't."

We had wasted so much time, each of us trying to bury what we felt instead of embracing what was there.

He lay down on the frozen ground. I curled up against his firm stomach, draping his heavy arm over my shoulders. The sunlight started to fade behind the trees while I listened to him breathe. My own breath came in short, frosted gasps. The pleasure of his kiss faded away, replaced by an ache so deep I could feel it in my bones.

A ring of silver stars appeared above us, glistening in the low light.

I felt his hold around me slacken, and the metal pelted my face, drawing pricks of blood.

His body was perfectly still other than the slow rise and fall of his chest. I turned into his chest, pressed my face to him, and just cried. Despair made me unable to move. So I closed my eyes and tried to doze under Xian's heavy fur.

If I gave Xian the heartstone and he took the power from the earth, would Pharo's connection to Faern break? Could he come back from this cursed sleep before the true end claimed him?

The thought gave me enough hope to sit up.

I traced Pharo's shadow beard with my finger. Would he forgive me if I gave the source of our magic to the enemy? Pharo might never understand. I knew that. If he'd been in my place, he would have fought relentlessly for Thim.

My death wouldn't have broken him or his resolve to serve our country. Maybe he was a better person than me, or maybe I simply loved him more.

Xian would use the pendant and give himself more power than any person had a right to command. I thought about all the power of all the inhabitors I'd ever known, the collective energy it must take to allow us to enter and control the bodies of other creatures, to experience their memories. If I told Xian where to find the pendant, all of that raw power would be his.

I wasn't sure I trusted him with that. He'd shown that he wanted to be merciful to the town's people, but his idea of mercy and mine were not the same. Was that the kind of ruler he'd be?

He believed in sacrificing people for the good of Myeik, for the sake of his family, for the security of the soldiers who fought for him.

In some ways, maybe he and Pharo weren't so different.

I imagined how Xian's handsome face would brighten with happiness, the way his deft and agile fingers would run over the surface of the pendant, revering it like a lover.

With Pharo's warmth still wet on my lips, I felt a little shiver of desire go through my chest, followed by a piercing stab of self-hatred so sharp it made another sob burst from my gut. I loved Pharo. I didn't love Xian, but still, some part of me wanted him, if only to ease the loneliness. I wanted his approval.

I stripped off my fur and spread it over Pharo. I had no hope of dragging his heavy body back to the monastery, but I was sure Ugyen would tell the rebels where to find him.

I didn't worry that they would kill him. That wasn't our custom. And they would do their best to care for him. Pharo was strong and fit. He would live through the slow starvation for weeks, maybe months. There would be enough time for me to free his soul from its tether to the heartstone.

I climbed to my feet and started jogging back into the forest.

Ugyen stepped out from behind a tree, holding the falcon on his arm.

He tried to put his arm around me, stripping his own heavy cloak and offering it to me. "You must be freezing…. Here, take this. I'll stay with him until others come to collect him."

"I said get away from me. What part of that didn't you understand?" I shouted. I pulled my fist back and hit him with all my strength. "How dare you follow me like that? And watch us…."

Ugyen pressed his hand to his cheek. He rubbed at the bruise forming under his eye. "Tashi…."

But I took off running and couldn't look back.

CHAPTER 12

I RAN until my tired legs buckled and I collapsed into a pile of fresh pine needles and snow. Folding my knees to my chest, I reached for Katala and found her dreaming.

I wanted to wake her, to make her shake Faern, bite him, anything to make the old wolf take one more gasping breath. But something in the dream vision made me pause. A sense of déjà vu came over me as I recognized the hazy memory swimming in my tiger's sleeping imagination.

Katala loomed over a deer carcass. Blood dripped down her jaw, staining her blonde fur the color of rust. But she wasn't interested in the meal. Her ears pricked up, and she focused her intense stare at a clearing in the trees. A soft singing drifted through her memory. The high childish voice stumbled over the words to the song.

I knew I should wake her. Asking our bonded why they had chosen us was forbidden, part of our ancient code, a preliminary exercise in self-control. It was for us to discover on our journey.

To ask why disturbs fate, Mistress Lhamo used to say. *The animal sees something in you that draws them, but as you bond, the thing that makes you successful as a pair may be something else entirely. Balance. At all times balance within yourself. Do not focus in on that one trait.*

But the things I'd been taught were wrong. I knew that now, and so I let her dream on as I watched.

Crouching low against the earth, Katala crept toward the source of the song. A small child sat on a rock, playing with a tattered owl doll. A sense of desire filled her, but it wasn't hunger or bloodlust. She hesitated, just watching the child who had been me fidget with nerves and sadness. Then she sprang, and I watched her tackle me and lick my hair for the first time.

Her dream shifted, and she was back in the river of her night visions, surrounded by a pair of cubs splashing. The cubs were older than I'd ever seen them in her dreams before. They were juveniles, with long legs, huge paws, and lithe with muscle. The male cub approached her, butting against her side. I'd seen her nurse the babies of her dreams before, but this time she pushed him away with a little growl. The cub blinked in confusion before trotting off to rejoin his sibling.

In a rush of understanding, it hit me. Katala hadn't chosen me for my strength or abilities like everyone at the academy thought. She'd chosen me because I was weak, a lonely cub calling out to her.

I watched the cubs wrestle on the river's bank. Katala stretched out in the sun and yawned.

The female cub bowled her brother over. He snarled as he splashed in water, lowering himself into a mimicked version of the tiger's lethal crouch. The cubs weren't babies anymore.

And neither was I. I wasn't brave, but I was learning to get past my fear.

Maybe when she'd selected me all those years ago, she'd known she could fix me. And maybe, like the cubs in her dreams, I would someday grow enough not to depend on her anymore. She hadn't chosen me because I was brave or strong or ready for the role Ugyen wanted me to grow into. She'd chosen me because I was fragile and she wasn't, and our relationship existed in balance.

But with Pharo gone, if I lost Katala too, I would truly be alone. Was I ready to take that step? Would I ever be?

WHEN I crept back to Xian's rooms, my eyes were still red from crying. To my dismay, Zeyar waited inside the chamber, perched on the edge of the large bed. But for once, the cranky steward's focus wasn't on me. Xian reclined against a mountain of pillows. His face was twisted with pain while the old monk from the infirmary wound strips of bandage cloth around his hip.

I'd heard something crack when Katala pounced, but in her body, the tackle had felt almost playful, light. I didn't stop to think how easily her weight and speed could hurt Xian when I'd tried to be gentle. In my own body, Xian seemed so solid and strong, but when faced with my tiger, he was as fragile as a porcelain doll.

When Xian moaned, panic swelled alongside guilt inside me. In the moment, I had barely thought about the consequences of my actions. All I'd known was the need to save Pharo. But now the whole Myeik army knew what Katala looked like. Xian knew what she looked like and knew what she was. They'd all be hunting her, and we no longer had the option of melting into the shadows. Worse, I couldn't stop the genuine guilt I felt over causing Xian pain.

If you tell him about the pendant, said a little voice in my head, *you'll lose your connection with her. She'll be free of you and this bond that holds her back. She can run. You could save her and Pharo.*

If you do it, said another voice, equally insidious, *you might never see either of them again. They'll be disgusted with you.*

"Where have you been?" Zeyar demanded. "The company has been back almost an hour. The commander needs tending, and I have a million things to do in the camp."

"I went for a walk," I stammered. Turning my back to him, I wiped my eyes again before unfastening the lock on the door and opening it. "You can go. I'll look after him."

"You don't dismiss me," Zeyar began. He jabbed his bony finger into my chest.

But Xian cleared his throat. "Your whining voice is going to put me into an early grave," he moaned, turning onto his side. "Leave us, Zeyar. I don't have the energy for you right now."

The steward flushed red, but he bowed to his commander and left the room without another word. Part of me wondered if Xian wasn't treading on dangerous ground by humiliating the old soldier. Zeyar had proven that he could carry a grudge. The old monk finished wrapping the commander's wound and dismissed himself wordlessly.

Belatedly, I reminded myself to act surprised. "What happened to you? Did you fall from your horse?"

Xian flashed me a half smile. "I was attacked by a giant tiger. I lived, and now I'm a legend among men."

"You killed it?"

"Nah. She ran away."

I raised an eyebrow, but inwardly I wondered if he was suspicious. Predators the size of Katala didn't just abandon easy prey like humans. "Just like that?"

"To be truthful, I have no idea why. I told the regiment she smelled the rage on me and knew I wasn't someone she wanted to trifle with. One of the cheekier infantrymen joked it was just the stench." He laughed, then groaned as he pushed himself upright on a stack of pillows. "I didn't fight her… we found that wolf in the woods, and she came to his aid. But it was almost as if she just wanted to push me away from it, not hurt me. I don't think I could have escaped if she'd wanted me dead."

I began stripping off my wet clothes. "Maybe she just wasn't hungry."

"Then why expose herself at all? It seems obvious she was controlled by something else. The wolf too." He pulled his blankets up to his chin and then sipped some of the tea Zeyar had left on his bedside table. "The wizard must be more powerful than we thought."

Leaving my overclothes in a heap by the door, I went to sit beside him wearing only the army-issue tunic. Little bumps dotted my thighs, and my hairs stood on end. While I was holding Pharo, I hadn't noticed the melting snow seeping through my furs to my skin. The panic of the situation, the rush to make it to him before it was too late, had kept me warm. Now the cold went right through me, closing its cruel fist around my raw heart.

Xian reached for the edge of my tunic. "This is damp. What were you doing? Rolling around in the creek?"

"I was sitting in the snow."

"Sitting in the snow?" He chuckled, then winced.

I tried to form words, grasping desperately to maintain the charade. But pure emotion burst out of my mouth instead of the lies I wanted to spin. A sob escaped. Others followed, until my vision blurred and my lungs fought for air.

He tossed off his blankets and pulled me into his chest with those impossibly strong arms, even though the action made him grimace with pain. Closing my eyes, I let the warm tears flow down my frozen cheeks.

I wished I could blame him for Pharo's death. It would have been easier to focus my hate on a single person, even if that person had his arms wrapped around my back. Instead, it was the lie of my whole life that had killed my best friend. Everyone we'd trusted to teach us, who had assured us there was no other way to harness Thim's lifeblood, was complicit in his death. Worse yet, so was I. I'd never thought to ask questions. I'd been naïve, complacent in the knowledge that a golden tiger had picked me and my death was a long way away.

I was still fighting for the sake of that lie.

When my crying subsided into whimpers, Xian whispered into my hair, "Tell me what this is about. Where did you go today?"

His breath felt warm and soothing against my ear, but his question made dread curdle inside me.

"I met a friend."

After a pause, he spoke again, and all the gentleness vanished from his voice. "What do you mean, 'you met a friend?' What friend? Who would you possibly go to meet in the woods?"

I knew I had to make a choice. If I told him about the pendant, about Pharo, then the fertile soils of Thim might dry up. No one could remember a drought, a plague, or a bad harvest in centuries of our history. Without the heartstone connected to our earth, how much of that would change? We would need the rich soil more than ever now with half of the country dead or carted away. But the pendant hadn't protected our borders from the Myeik's soldiers. It hadn't stopped them from raiding our temples, enslaving our people, and burning our crops to the ground. The natural wealth of our land drew them to our borders like bees to a pot of honey.

If the state of the capitol was anything to go by, then my country was gone, reduced to ash and fields and husks of buildings filled with starved corpses.

If I told Xian about the tree, all the inhabitors I knew would have a chance at a real and full life—human and beast. We would no longer be sacrifices to Ugyen's ancient idea of balance.

I pinched the bridge of my nose. If I was brutally honest with myself, there were only two beings I cared about saving. Whatever happened with Xian, whatever I became to him, I needed Pharo to live, and I wanted Katala to have the cubs she saw in her dreams.

A void of sadness stopped the flow of tears. The strength of it drew all my emotion inward into a numb abyss. I might never see either of them again, but they'd be happy. They would live.

Slowly, I lifted my gaze to look into Xian's eyes. A storm grew in those ocean-colored orbs. Hiding my face in his neck, pressing my lips to the curve of his chin like a lover, I whispered, "I know where your pendant is."

His jaw went slack. "And you'll tell me?"

I nodded.

For a moment, he just stared at me, eyes sparkling with wonder and a kind of childlike, innocent hope. Then they narrowed again and he snapped, "Why would you tell me that? I'm not sure how that knowledge came to you, but why would you tell me? I'm an invader. And you can't think me so naïve as to believe you've come to care for me so much that you would give your country's last weapon to the enemy."

When he phrased it like that, I shivered. It wasn't too late to take my choice back. I still had time to reconsider. But then I thought back to that night in the crypts, when I'd taken notes for Xian as he tried to beat the truth from Ugyen's lips. I'd seen glimpses of Xian's vulnerability, his capacity for mercy and kindness, but I'd seen something darker inside him too. Something that enjoyed the pain he caused. I didn't know if I could be as brave as Ugyen in the face of his sadism. And now that he knew the secret I carried, I was sure he would beat it out of me if necessary.

Once he had the pendant, which side of his personality would rule it? The gentle boy who loved his mother and covered me with an extra fur while I slept, or the monster who cut a line down an old monk's belly? What would my role be in the new world he could create?

But my choice wasn't for him. I needed to do this or I'd bury any chance of seeing Pharo again.

I shook my head. "You don't understand."

Xian went very quiet. His eyes bored into mine, and he seemed to study me as questions churned in his mind.

I expected a flood of demands. Instead, he leaned toward me, and for the second time that day, I felt a pair of moist lips brush against mine. His kiss was firmer than Pharo's, more confident and more insistent. His fingers moved up my tunic, and his nails raked my back. A moan escaped my lips as all my senses exploded in need. I loved someone else, but I wanted him on an animalistic level I didn't quite understand.

I'd never felt more like a traitor, but the sin tasted like cinnamon and sweet rice with milk.

Then he pulled me into his chest, but the strength of his grip was possessive and doubt crashed over me. He was acting as if I belonged to him. He hadn't even asked me before he claimed my lips.

The anger resurfaced. I slipped from his grasp and scooted away until my back pressed against the wall.

"Wait," he said. "Wait. I didn't mean to scare you. I'm sorry. I… I thought you would want that. I've noticed the way you look at me."

"Do I have a choice?"

"What?"

"I need to know. Can I refuse you? Can I say no without there being consequences? And more, can I choose to stay here when you leave?" My voice rose higher and higher until I was shouting at him.

"They treat you horribly here—when we first came—"

I cut him off. "That isn't what I'm asking."

He sighed and looked down, picking at the edge of his blanket. "If you want to leave when the army moves on, you can go. I told you that at the beginning."

"You're saying you don't own me?"

"I don't own you," he repeated, voice heavy with emotion. "But I don't really want to lose you either."

"And what if I decide not to tell you where it is after all? Or what if I'm wrong?" I raised my chin and set my jaw. My voice threatened to break again. "Will you hurt me? Will you torture me like you did Ugyen?"

"No." His eyes went hard again. "How can you even think that?"

"I've changed my mind," I whispered, because I had to know, really *know*, that he could accept my decision before I could go through with giving him what he wanted, before I could entrust him with any more power. "I don't want to tell you. I can't do this."

Xian closed his eyes, and I hated the look of anguish on his face before he closed off his emotions. "My mother—"

"I know," I said. "I read your letter."

He drew a sharp breath. Then, before I could respond, he got to his feet. Clutching his wound, he limped to the door and wrenched it open. "Get out. Take whatever is yours and leave."

I took a step toward him and reached for his clammy hand.

"Don't." All the command and confidence had gone from his voice. A single tear leaked from under his heavy lashes, and he blushed with shame.

I brushed the tear away with my fingers. "I'll show you."

"What?" he asked, anger and suspicion creeping into his tone again.

"A test," I said, shutting the door and turning him to face me. "You passed."

THE MONASTERY bells tolled seven, marking the time of my betrayal. Xian and I battled through a stream of novices heading to the refectory. While they'd never looked overweight, I noticed gaunt shadows on the boys' cheeks, and collarbones that protruded. Hosting an army, even a small company like Xian's, was taking its toll on Chirang's resources. I wondered how much longer they'd be able to survive like this.

Once the boys noticed Xian's face and the golden badge pinned to his chest, they gave us a wide berth, parting around us like a school of fish. He reached out and took my hand. At first I stiffened, feeling the eyes of the novices immediately snap to our clasped fingers. But after a moment, I relaxed. Considering what I was about to do, it hardly mattered what they thought now. Xian's callused fingers gently stroked my palm.

Even as a warm, tingling feeling shot up my back, I thought of Pharo and wished it was his hand instead.

The courtyard was empty and silent, but still I couldn't help holding my breath as we stepped from the wooden dais onto the crisp grass. Despite all the lies I'd been told at the academy, if I gave Xian the pendant now there would be no going back. But since arriving at the monastery, I'd had almost no news of the state of Jakar. If the Dzong had fallen, then the whole city might lie in broken pieces and scattered ash.

"It's here?" Xian whispered.

I nodded, and he squeezed my hand. My palm was sweaty despite the cold, but his touch made my fingers feel numb. I wanted freedom, for myself and everyone else I knew who were bound to a short life serving a country that no longer existed. More than anything, I wanted the chance to see Pharo again, even if he hated me.

I led Xian to the very center of the garden, to the base of the cherry tree. Tonight it bloomed white, with delicate flowers perfuming the wind that bit my cheeks and lips. Part of me expected the pendant itself to rebel. Surely an object so powerful wouldn't allow itself to be dug out and passed to another? Surely it would fight back against my arrogance. I waited for pain as I stepped forward and laid my hand on the tree's frosted trunk.

I felt only rough bark and melting snow. "It's here," I said, my voice barely audible over the wind.

A falcon's high-pitched cry pierced the air. A second later, I had to duck as Ugyen's bird dove toward my face, talons poised. I imagined the old monk's anger driving her, intent on tearing out my eyes and devouring them. Xian pulled his broadsword from his belt and swung at the white shadow that swooped toward me again. His blade missed, but the flat collided with the falcon's wing with enough power to make her shriek.

"I won't miss next time," Xian growled, knuckles going white around the sword's jeweled hilt. The falcon shook its snowy head and then disappeared into the sky, blending into the moonlight.

I rose from my crouch. Xian's hands were on the tree's trunk, stroking it and speaking gently like he would do with a frightened horse. "It seems so obvious," he said. "A cherry tree that blooms outside in weather like this? Blossoms that change color with the day...."

I nodded, licking my wind-chapped lips.

He sighed and leaned against the tree. "Getting it without anyone else important in the army noticing will be difficult. It'll have to be done fast."

"Do many of them know about the pendant?"

"It's a legend," he said. "Many of us from the lakes region grow up hearing about it. Before we lost it, the region was fertile and rich with minerals—the wealthiest in the country. Now the lakes die a little more each year. Our crops don't thrive, and some types won't grow at all. But they also know that it was my family who controlled it, and we weren't always benevolent."

I shuddered, wondering if everyone in his family was like him, kind one moment, violent the next. I could understand why people would fear a ruler like that.

"I don't dare leave the tree." Xian sat on the earth, laying his sword across his lap. "That falcon was human. She knew what you were about to show me. Who is to say that the wizard she serves won't come back and take the pendant before I can get to it?"

"I wouldn't know who to bring," I said, picking at the hem of my tunic. "Not Zeyar, surely."

Xian laughed. "Zeyar? I wouldn't trust him to brush my horse if I had a choice. General Liu assigned him to me, and I have to keep up appearances. She uses him to keep tabs on my whereabouts."

"She doesn't trust you?"

"Our families have a long history. I don't think Liu trusts anybody." He stood back up and paced around the base of the tree. "Where is the stone? Inside, underneath?"

I still didn't dare try to connect with him watching me. Part of me still believed that he would slay me on the spot if he learned the truth about what I was, even though I was betraying the inhabitors' greatest secret. Racking my memory for those hazy pictures conjured amid the incense with Ugyen, I said, "Inside. I don't know where, though."

He ran his fingers up and down the tree's bark. "How did they get it in there, I wonder?"

"Maybe it grew alongside the tree. You said your family lost it a thousand years ago. As far as I know, Chirang is almost that old." Now that I'd betrayed them, it was strange how easily my people's history flowed from my tongue.

He paused, feeling out a knot in the middle of the trunk. A few downy feathers and pine needles lined the inside of the small hole, the abandoned home of a pair of sparrows or a robin. I was light-headed with relief—my uncertainty dimming with each passing moment. Pharo would come back.

Suddenly he pulled his hand back. Hissing in pain, he clutched it to his chest. "It's hot," he said breathlessly. "Scalding like boiling water."

Maybe the stone had decided to fight back after all.

He slid his sword hilt into the tree's knot until it touched the back. Then he swiveled it around. His tongue poked out of his mouth as he concentrated. But I didn't hear the chink of metal meeting metal, and when he pulled the sword back, his face fell.

Turning the sword over in his hand, he sighed again. "I really like this sword. The wood will ruin it."

Then he drew his shoulder back and drove it into the trunk with all his strength. Splinters of wood broke off, shattering the snow-covered ground as Xian grunted and swung.

"Should you be doing that with your injury?" I asked.

Xian shrugged. "I don't trust anyone else."

Sweat oozed down his forehead, and he moaned with effort. A group of novices appeared on the fringe of the courtyard, huddling together and whispering. A moment later, a few of Xian's personal guard rushed into the gardens, surrounding the tree.

A burly soldier with so much chest hair it stuck out around his collar stepped around me and approached Xian. "Commander, sir, please allow me to fetch an ax and complete this task for you...."

"No!" Xian snapped. "Get back with the others. I will do this."

The man stepped away. No one else dared to come forward.

He wiped the sweat away with his sleeve, sniffling as the cold air made his nose run. Turning to me briefly, he smiled. He had a gleam in his eyes, the same kind of glittering madness I'd seen in them on the night he tortured Ugyen.

What had I done? I tried to force the feelings of guilt away. I'd known how much he wanted this. He would be taking the pendant far away—too far for any consequences of his tyranny to be felt here. His cut in the tree's slender trunk steadily deepened.

More snow began to fall like ash all around us as more novices and soldiers gathered in the courtyard to watch their commander hack the tree. Part of me wanted to retreat, to back away from all their attention and scorn. But my feet were frozen in place, and there was no one I could go to for comfort.

Pulling his sleeve over his hand, he reached deep into the trunk again. My headache began to sear as Katala desperately fought to open our connection. Her fear was so strong I could nearly feel it in the air. The magic almost seemed to seep out through my pores. Then, abruptly, the headache stopped. Emptiness made me shake.

Xian yelped in triumph and pulled his arm out of the tree. A golden chain dangled from his closed fist. The pendant was the size of a goose egg, a dark ruby set in a circlet of gold and diamonds.

With shaking fingers, he lifted the pendant by the chain and hung it around his neck. He took my arm and squeezed it. The madness had gone from his eyes, replaced by liquid warmth. "Come. Let's go in out of the snow. We've given them enough to speculate over, and I need to make travel plans. Once they learn what I have, the leaders of my own army will try to kill me. But once I'm home, they won't manage it."

I nodded and tried to smile for him. He slipped his arm through mine, and we walked slowly back to the dais, weaving through the assembled crowd.

Ugyen stood against one of the wooden columns. The falcon perched on his bare arm, her talons digging into his flesh so deeply that blood dripped down into the snow. She crowed and clacked her beak in distress. A hot pool of red splashed Ugyen's bare feet.

"I can't feel her," he whispered, shivering and looking up at the sky. He started rocking back and forth on the balls of his feet. "I can't feel her."

I tried to brush past him, clinging to Xian for safety. But his arm darted out, and he clawed at the edge of my tunic. "Please. Make this right. You're the only one who still can."

CHAPTER 13

XIAN WASTED no time in summoning his steward to help him pack up his things in the abbot's chamber. As soon as we walked in the door, he put his head outside and barked to the guard who stood at the entrance to the chapel. After what he'd told me about Zeyar, I wondered if he did this on purpose, to keep the old man from relaying what he'd seen to General Liu. If he kept Zeyar in his sights, then the troublesome steward wouldn't be able to send a message.

But if Zeyar had questions about his commander's swift departure, he had the sense to keep them to himself. When he arrived, shuffling through the door wearing his classic scowl, the steward immediately began dragging boxes from the wardrobe, organizing the commander's clothing and possessions. He didn't comment as Xian issued terse commands or complain at having to hurry. While the steward carefully folded his linens, Xian started wiping down his weapon with fervor. He paused only to toss his old sword across the room in disgust when he examined the state of the blunt edge.

I lay down on Xian's bed, folding myself into the fetal position. I clutched a pillow to my chest as I tried to reach for Katala. My head didn't swim or pound. I felt nothing except the downy pillow clasped in my fingers and the steady heat emitted by the fire. My body felt heavier, more solid than it had in years, as if I gained another person in weight the instant Xian put the heartstone around his neck. But everything else seemed dulled. I couldn't smell the textures of the air. When I tried to watch Zeyar across the room, I realized that his outline was blurry.

"Isn't Tashi going to help?" the steward demanded.

Xian glanced up at me and then shrugged. "If they want to. Get this done quickly. I want everything to be ready by the morning. When you finish here, alert my guard to be ready to move, with our horses ready."

"If they want to," the old steward mimicked and then scoffed.

"Excuse me?" Xian's voice was low and dangerous. I sat up, a small seed of pleasure blossoming in my stomach as I imagined Xian punching Zeyar in the jaw.

The steward threw down an armful of clothes. "Why am I even here? As soon as the general hears what you've found, she's going to come after you. She'll gut you to get it. She has to. Not that she'll need the pretense. We all know that her word is law over you until you reach home."

Xian crossed the room in three long strides. Holding his dagger to Zeyar's throat, he whispered, "No matter where your allegiances lie, I am your commander until the moment I leave this camp, and if I tell you to pack the bags, you will do it."

"You're deserting us." Zeyar barked a laugh. "Surely I can't be hauled before a tribunal for refusing to aid a deserter?"

Fury flashed through Xian's eyes, and for a moment, I wondered if he would actually slit Zeyar's throat. Without moving his dagger, Xian fished inside his furs and drew out a letter. "As you well know, when General Liu pretended to be concerned for my fitness as a result of my mother's illness, she gave me open-ended license to travel home. I'm making use of that now. Do what I tell you, or in my last minutes as your commander, I will court-martial you."

Zeyar shivered.

Xian lowered his head, brushing his lips up against the steward's ear before hissing, "Or I'll cut your throat right here. I'm sure the Thim you hate so much will help me mop your blood off the floor."

Zeyar's shoulders went slack, and his face turned the color of boiled rice. He shook his head and backed away from Xian's knife. Kneeling to pick up the clothes he'd dropped, he muttered, "No, Commander, sir... that will not be necessary."

Xian straightened and went back to cleaning his weapons.

I rolled onto my back, staring at the engraved ceiling. The Ghungza's cracked marble face stared back at me with disapproval. Everything was happening so quickly, and I still had to decide whether to stay here or leave with Xian. If Ugyen was anything to judge by, the other inhabitors would hate me and condemn me. But what of the ones I'd brought back? What would they think when they awoke from their coma and realized they never had to die?

If I left now, I'd have no chance to see Pharo again. No chance to try to explain everything.

Xian lifted the first of his heavy saddlebags from the ground and swung it effortlessly over his shoulder, as if the weapons weighed no more than cotton. He motioned for Zeyar to grab another. "Let's go take this lot down to the camp. I don't trust you alone in a room with just Tashi, so you'll come too."

The steward lifted another bag, grunting with effort. He didn't try to protest or argue with Xian again. Following the commander as meekly as a spaniel pup, Zeyar pulled the door tight behind them, leaving me to think.

As soon as their footsteps died down the hallway, someone knocked on the door. A knot of fear formed in my stomach, and I reached under Xian's pillow for the extra dagger he kept there. If Ugyen was at the door, I didn't dare face him unarmed. But the weapon felt foreign in my grasp. I was used to Katala's claws and her knifelike teeth. Could I even use a weapon like this? I'd come last in every hand-to-hand combat class in the academy.

I unfastened the lock and pushed the door open just a crack. Before I had a chance to look outside, a strong arm shoved the oak door open with enough force to send me teetering backward. I landed hard on the wood floor, cracking my head against one of Xian's trunks.

Pharo stepped through onto the landing. He was dressed simply in a peasant's pale, undyed wool. The clothes were too big for him and drowned him in white like a ghost. But his dark eyes glowed bright with life.

He extended his hand to help me to my feet. Part of me expected him to pick me up just so he could punch me onto the floor again. Instead he dragged me to his chest, crushing my ribs in a tight hug. I savored the warmth of him. His smell was different now, but without Katala's heightened senses, I couldn't tell if he had changed or if it was the change in me. I lifted my chin to sniff the hollow of his throat. I brushed my cheek against the feather-soft brown skin. When he didn't push me away, I surprised myself by pressing a kiss to his jaw.

Instantly, I tried to pull away, embarrassed. Our kiss by the stream was something I had to forget now that he would live. Especially since I'd betrayed him in more ways than one. We had to push past whatever had happened between us there, if we would even have a chance at reclaiming our friendship. I was sure he hadn't meant what he'd said. His words had only been to comfort me when I needed them the most.

He hugged me tighter, half lifting me off my feet. I could feel the sheer strength of him, a bearlike, raw power compared to Xian's more feline sinuousness. Then he leaned down and kissed me.

The kiss was not like our last. It was tender, exploratory, and slow. He teased me, letting our tongues meet and then shying away. The stubble on his chin rubbed rough against my skin. The strength of his arms around me continued to drive the air from my lungs, but the kiss itself was gentle—so gentle, and full of promise. I felt feminine in his arms, and I wondered if that was how he thought of me too. Warm tears slid down my lashes.

I had questions for him, but they could wait. I clamped my legs tight around his waist and let him carry me to Xian's bed. I knew Xian and Zeyar could come back and find us like this, but when he laid me down on the thick furs and slipped my tunic over my head, I was past caring.

His lithe fingers gripped my hips. His lips traveled to the edge of my jaw, and he nipped along my neck like a wolf would do, his teeth leaving imprints that burned me with pleasure. I curled my arms around his neck, moaning when he kissed down the trail of hair leading from my navel.

Every inch of my skin seemed to breathe with its own life. How long had I wanted this? How could I have thought that a stolen kiss with Xian could soothe even part of Pharo's loss?

His lips brushed against the waistband of my trousers, and his fingers worked the buttons open. I pushed them down past my ankles, desperate to feel his skin against my thighs. Chuckling, he ran the edge of his finger down my leg, letting it trail slowly until my hips bucked up of their own accord.

"Pharo," I said urgently. I'd never done this before.

But then his mouth closed around me and I drowned—lost to the sensuous warmth, pleasure, and a flood of emotion.

I TRACED the dark hair around his jaw, my body pressed against his. I hoped Xian would get caught up at the camp forever, but I knew this game we were playing, where it was safe to lie here in each other's arms, couldn't last. "How did you know to come here?"

"Ugyen sent for me right away when the bond broke. He wanted me to talk sense into you. Get you to steal it back while he sleeps or something," he said, releasing me. He had a sheepish look on his face, and he studied his feet. "I haven't made up my mind about that."

"What did they tell you?" I murmured against his sweaty chest.

He shrugged. "As much as they could in the past hour, really. The camp is split. There are some who are calling you a traitor. Lots of those. But others, even if they don't agree with what you did, they've seen so many of their friends die young when all this time it didn't have to be that way. They're angry too, but not at you."

Pharo swallowed hard and pawed at the tears forming in his eyes. I didn't even bother to try to mop the dampness on my face.

"What do you think about it?"

"Well, I'm glad to be alive, but I don't know, Tashi... giving something that powerful to our enemies...." His brows knitted together, and he studied me at arm's length. "Whatever people like

Ugyen have kept from us, we still have a duty. We still have to protect the people who live here."

"The heartstone didn't protect us from invasion," I snapped. He sounded like Ugyen, like Mistress Lhamo. But both of them were wrong. "It didn't stop them from blowing cannons through our city walls and starving the city's officials until we surrendered. And it didn't stop them from sending half the city's population to the auction block."

"We have no idea what that pendant could have done if we knew how to really use it." Pharo took me by both shoulders. "All these centuries, inhabitors have been tasked with monitoring the flow of power. We connect with nature. We monitor the weather, and our steps leave fertile soil in our wake. Before today, most of us never had a clue where our power came from. We still don't know how it works or what it can do. We've been limited all this time. We're taught a few simple things at the academy, but we don't learn many spells. We don't learn how to actually exercise any of that power. I think it can do so much more than we know."

"Ugyen will never tell me," I said. "I was supposed to be the guardian. He said he would have shared its secrets over years with me. He'll never trust me with any of that now."

"Maybe there are things Ugyen doesn't even know. He said the commander's ancestors used it. Maybe we can learn from them how to make it work. They must know where it came from, who made it."

"You think Xian will just tell me how it works?"

"He trusts you, doesn't he?"

I barked a laugh. "As much as he trusts anyone, but I don't think that says very much, Pharo."

"You could continue to spy. Go with him."

I stared at him. "And then what? Steal it back from him? Use it to put the country back together?"

"You're a trained spy, Tashi. That hasn't changed. That wasn't a lie."

"I was trained to spy at a distance! To see what Katala saw. That's all gone now."

"You don't need Katala to do this! You're the one that monster trusts! You can do this."

I pushed away from him and got up from the bed. I tried to process everything he was asking of me. Seeing him alive, knowing that he didn't hate me... I didn't want to leave him. Now that we were unbound, love became possible. A life beyond our duty and the academy became possible. Even though I felt hollow without Katala, a life with Pharo could heal that void.

But what about all those inhabitors who thought I was a traitor? How long would I live if I stayed? Xian had never hurt me. He promised that I could go home whenever I desired. But he was dangerous, and I knew without any doubt that he would kill me if I stole from him.

"You want me to leave everything behind? To go to Myeik alone?"

"Come on, Tash. I'll find a way to come with you. We'll matter." Pharo flashed me a little smile. He wrapped both arms around my back.

"You always mattered to me!" Emotion made my hands curl into fists. I banged them on his chest as tears started to fall. "Always! I've killed for you."

He nodded and then looked down. "I know. But this place is our home. We have to do something to save it."

"This place, these people—our home—abandoned us, lied to us, and sacrificed us. What right do any of them have to demand more?"

"So you're happy to just let them take all of us as slaves? Put us to work in the mines? Is that it? Even the children?" Pharo reached for his clothes and started tugging them back on.

"No," I snapped. My thoughts traveled back to the village at the foot of the mountain, to the people huddled against the wall in fear, and the child.... "I didn't say that."

I heard footsteps outside and Xian's voice directing a group of soldiers.

Pharo glanced at the door. He rose and opened it but hesitated in the frame as I scrambled for my clothes. "Fuck Ugyen and

Mistress Lhamo. They're two liars out of everyone we've known. Everyone else was deceived like we were, and many of them died supporting that lie. Do this for everyone else. I will follow you. I will help you. I promise."

He slipped outside into the night as a protest died on my tongue. My mouth still tasted of him.

WE LEFT at dawn, while the sun cast purple shadows over the mountainside. I rode behind Xian on his stallion, my arms wrapped around his waist. The pendant swung from his neck, peeking out from under his white traveling cloak and glittering when the sunlight caught it. His guards flanked our horse, each of them mounted on steady pack animals instead of the flashy mounts I'd seen them ride around the camp.

Descending the slope, we passed an elephant skull, stripped bare in weeks by the winds and hungry predators looking for an easy meal. So much had changed in the last few weeks, but here I was, running away again.

We rode in silence. Whenever one of the guards tried to strike up conversation, Xian turned in the saddle and held his finger to his lips. "Not until we get out in the open," he whispered. "The rebels could be anywhere. They'll know what I have, and they won't want me to get over the border with it."

The guards seemed to accept this explanation, not knowing that the source of the rebels' real power hung around their commander's neck. Based on the conversation he'd had with Zeyar the night before, I assumed he feared General Liu and how fast her scouts might search us out, more than any lingering militia in the mountains.

It didn't take long for the wind to penetrate my heavy furs. Our pace was slow, and even with Xian's body heat pressed against me, the farther we descended, the steeper the mountain's slope became and the harder the wind hit us. The trees thinned, and the pitted, rocky cliffs provided no shelter.

Xian looked over his shoulder at me, laughing. "Don't worry. Where we're going, it's hot enough to bake bricks outside in the sun. You'll never feel cold like this again."

"Unless I decide to return," I said quickly.

He sighed, rolling his eyes. His cockiness made me want to dismount and run back to Pharo, our magic and the rest of the inhabitors be damned. "Yes, unless you decide to return."

As we neared the foothills, I looked down on the village we'd searched looking for Chen. It slept peacefully, with smoke rising from the houses' chimneys, the rice fields covered in mist. Horses and goats browsed the grass in the lush pastures, tails flickering. Everything looked crisp and green, ready to awaken from frosted sleep with the sun.

"You didn't burn it," I whispered, stunned.

A smile twitched at the corners of his mouth. "No."

The stallion slid a few feet, grunting as he rebalanced himself under our shared weight. I remembered this part of the previous journey, galloping full throttle with the cliffs on either side. Xian leaned down to pat the horse's neck.

A sword swung over his lowered head. The blade narrowly missed my cheek.

Xian spun the stallion around. The horse's front feet lifted off the ground, and he pivoted so fast I almost flew from the saddle.

One of his guards braced his sword and kicked his horse forward. His hands trembled on the reins, and his eyes widened in fear. He'd missed his chance to kill Xian easily, and he knew it.

The other guards circled around him from behind, cutting off any escape.

"You *dare* to strike at me?" Xian roared, pulling his new sword from his belt. I'd never seen Xian in combat before. My grip around his waist tightened as I readied myself for the stallion's charge.

"She sent a falcon…. She asked me to do it." The guard's fingers trembled on his reins.

Xian's hand went to his neck. He ran his fingers over the pendant as if to make sure it was still there.

Lifting his shaking sword, the guard nudged his horse toward his commander, eyes closed as if bracing for death.

All around us, the ground started vibrating. Rocks tumbled down the cliffside. The horses reared, fighting to free their heads and run. Then a pine tree shot up from the earth under the terrified guard's horse, stabbing through the animal's belly like a giant stake as the rider screamed. Then the tree pierced through his body, tearing him open and growing to the sky. Terror impaled me as well. How did Xian know those spells? How long had he been studying and learning, just waiting for his chance to wield the heartstone's power?

The other guards kicked their horses and galloped down the mountain toward the village. My chest constricted and terror left me unable to breathe. Why wasn't I running too?

When I looked at Xian, he smiled.

"It knows me," he said. "The heartstone was meant to be with a warrior. It's been bored for too long."

I HUDDLED in my bedroll, trying not to cough as the fire-smoke stung my eyes and lungs. Xian sprawled out beside me, dead to the world while his remaining guards took it in turns to stir the fire and keep watch. We'd caught up with them at the village. Xian had acted equally surprised and fearful of the earthquake and his guard's impalement, but when their backs were turned his smile ate up his entire face.

Xian rolled toward me in the darkness. He wrapped his arms around my body and buried his face in my back. When I didn't protest, he planted a kiss on my shoulder. He sighed with contentment and drifted to sleep again, breath slow and hot.

In my terror, I wanted nothing more than to reach for Katala. I wanted my mind to be somewhere else, and I wanted her reassurance. Instead, even with Xian curling around me, I felt completely alone.

I forced myself to relax, trying to banish the image of the guard's split body and the sound of his dying screams. Xian had never hurt me, and after everything I'd said to him, I had no reason to believe he ever would.

Unless I stole the thing he wanted above everything else.

I turned over, resting my head on his limp arm. The ruby pendant blinked back at me from its spot, suspended in the middle of his chest—above his heart, which was fitting.

Reaching out, I brushed its warm surface with my fingertips. As soon as Xian had grasped it, the gem had cooled, almost as if it consciously accepted its fate with him. Or recognized the descendant of its rightful owner. And Xian himself had said the gem was bored.... I shuddered. The idea that the stone could think, that it had its own agenda, was even more terrifying than the thought of Xian controlling it.

A shock went through me, and a familiar headache pulsed at my temple as I held on to the stone. I pulled my hand back, shaking. I was sure that Xian would feel the energy that traveled from the pendant to me. But his eyes stayed closed and his chest rose in a steady rhythm.

Moving slowly, I dared to wrap my hand around the gem. The headache exploded; it felt like a knife pierced my skull. I closed my eyes, focused all the energy I had, and reached for Katala.

Xian snorted in his sleep. Was he aware of me? Could he feel that I was trying to reach someone? I'd been connected to the pendant all my life and never sensed its presence. Now I could feel its power channeling through me, making me dizzy. A little shiver went up my back as a single silver stone drifted up into the air above me. The connection was weak, but somewhere, deep inside my gut, I felt Katala's roar.

ACKNOWLEDGMENTS

THE IDEA for *The Tiger's Watch* came to me on a trip with my family. We'd just left Bhutan—a small country in the heart of the Himalayan mountains. Even more so than *Unicorn Tracks*, I think this series has a deep sense of place. I have to thank my dad for that and so many other things. Without him, I wouldn't have seen the world. Some of the best memories of my life happened while traveling with my family. Thank you for the memories and for expanding my worldview.

Thank you to the real Tashi, our supremely patient guide in Bhutan, for showing us his country and helping us fall in love with it. I am positive he was often frustrated with the fat American tourists who thought a gentle hike was a mountain climb and got food poisoning from holy water (that he told us not to drink), but he never showed it.

I also want to thank a few people who have been instrumental in helping *The Tiger's Watch* see publication:

To Carrie DiRisio, Jessica Gunn, Nina Rossing, and KT Hanna: Thank you for reading snippets of this book as I wrote and giving me so much needed encouragement to finish.

To Meghan Moss, my ever-amazing cover artist: I wouldn't have thought it was possible for you to top your design for *Unicorn Tracks*, but then you did. Your cover is a magnificent work of art, and I hope my words live up to it.

To Elizabeth, Anne, Dawn, Naomi, and the rest of the team at Harmony Ink Press: thank you for believing in me and my books! I am so excited to be working on another series with you.

Finally, thank you to my readers, especially those who have stuck with me through multiple books. In particular, I want to thank a few bloggers who have helped me SO MUCH in spreading the word about my books: Jamie and Dani (I had to group you two together. YOU KNOW I HAD TO), Olivia, Silvana, Mana, Nori, Jen, Avery, Nicole, Mish, Chelsea, Jacquie, and Amy.

Exclusive Excerpt

The Shadow Wolf

Ashes of Gold: Book Two

By Julia Ember

While the war in Thim continues to rage, seventeen-year-old spy Pharo isn't sure how to keep fighting. After losing his magic and his bonded wolf, he feels powerless in the face of the invasion. His home city has been destroyed. The rebel force is crumbling. Worst of all, his best friend is in the hands of the enemy.

Determined to keep his promise to Tashi and rescue them at all costs, Pharo forges an uneasy alliance with a shapeshifting enemy bounty hunter. Although she's brutal and morally questionable, Niang wants what Pharo does—to reclaim the magic pendant Xian stole and free those under his tyrannical rule.

Dragged into a foreign country and a new court, Pharo must learn to spy without magic and pray that his skills are enough to save his friend.

Coming Soon to
www.harmonyinkpress.com

CHAPTER 1

THE WOLF

EVEN THOUGH I clutched an iron pike, I felt about as dangerous as a day-old hound. The weapon glimmered in the strip of moonlight that bled between the pine trees, its blade sharp enough to maim with the softest kiss. I balanced on one foot, struggling not to shake, holding the long pike outstretched and steady, even though my shoulder ached under the weight. I inhaled a ragged breath. The frozen air made my lungs scream, but the pain was strangely comforting. It drowned out loss and grief—gave me focus.

"Pharo," the training master barked. He wove in and out of the row of students and adjusted clumsy stances with impatient taps from his riding crop. He came to stand behind me. I almost cringed, waiting for the stinging smack and the command to "lift your foot higher" or the cut of one of his shrewder insults. Instead, he motioned me forward.

I put my foot down with a relieved sigh. The other students turned to stare.

"Who told you that you could stop?" Master Gyann shouted at the others. The training master put his hands menacingly on his sword belt. The other students hastily returned to their practice. "Stillness and control. These are the things that will make you strong now that your magic has failed you. Sonam, come here."

An infantryman stepped toward us from the shadow of the trees. One of Gyann's surviving goons. I remembered the training master's guards from the academy, all of them silent and still as breathing stone, resplendent in their ceremonial golden armor. The infantryman had abandoned his city glamour. Sonam wore only homespun cloth and a jerkin of time-softened leather. His face was the mask of granite I remembered. He held only a simple wooden staff, not much wider than an old man's walking stick. But his innocuous choice of weapon scared me more than if he'd wielded a broadsword dipped in tar and fire. He was a man who knew he didn't need iron or bronze to defend himself.

I swallowed. I wasn't exactly small. When most people met me, they thought I was in my early twenties at least, instead of seventeen. But Sonam was a mountain. He towered over me by a head, his body swollen with bulging muscle and purple veins.

Sonam sank into a crouch. He tapped his bladeless staff against the frozen ground, a feral grin forming dimples that looked out of place on his broad face. I sighed and slipped into place a few feet from him. I could already feel spectral bruises on my thighs and back. Gyann's men were fast and lethal. And the old bastard loved pitting them against trainees. I didn't bother to ask for a blunted weapon. I'd never manage to hit Sonam anyway.

"Begin," Gyann said.

I hesitated for only a second, then lunged forward. Better to take my bruises and get this over with. Gyann wouldn't stop the fight until one of us was flat on our back. Dancing around Sonam in circles might buy me a few pain-free minutes, but ultimately it wouldn't save me. Gyann wanted me to attack.

Sonam dodged me. My pike thrust into the ground where his foot had been only a second before. He pivoted, moving faster than a man his size should have been able. Like a dancing bear, I thought, almost laughing aloud, before the butt of his staff connected with my side. I doubled over, holding my stomach. I dropped my pike, but Sonam just kept circling me.

"Pick it up!" Gyann clapped his hands.

I stole a glance at one of the other trainees, Bhutar. He grimaced with sympathy but didn't move from the stork position. We'd known each other all our lives and come back from death together when the bonds broke, but no one was going to risk Gyann's wrath by intervening. I noticed Bhutar's arm had started to tremble.

"Pick it up!" Gyann roared again, advancing on me and shoving me forward into the dirt.

I dropped to my knees, but somehow my hand found the grip on the pike. I lifted it and staggered back to my feet. Sonam raised his arms and twirled, as if beckoning to an invisible crowd. I wondered if he'd been a ring fighter in his life before. Most of Gyann's men came from the lower city. They were hardened men: thieves, criminals, professional assassins, spared prison in exchange for their service to the inhabitors at the academy. Not that there were any prisons left anymore. I didn't know why most of the men stuck around.

I lowered my eyes, hunched my shoulders, and took the smallest of steps back. In all my years bonded to Faern, my wolf had taught me a lot about body language. I knew how to make myself look small and submissive. Sonam tilted his head and laughed, still playing to a crowd only he could see. All the other students kept their eyes carefully trained on the dirt. At least they pretended not to watch my humiliation. Sonam cradled his arms and made a cooing noise at me. Good. Let him think I was afraid. At least deception was something I was still good at.

Then, in a burst of speed, I lunged. Sonam caught my eye at the last second, sensing, too late, what I was about to do. He stumbled backward and his foot caught on a tree root. As he scrambled for balance, I pounced on him, whacking his shin with the blunt side of the pike's blade.

Sonam snarled as he climbed to his feet. Tossing his weapon aside, he grabbed me by the neck. His callused fingers closed around my windpipe. I kicked, flailing like a fish on a hook as he lifted me into the air by the throat. My weapon dropped uselessly to the ground.

"You think because you're bigger than the rest of this pathetic lot that you're anything against me?" he hissed. I choked and kicked desperately against his rock-hard stomach.

"Enough, Sonam," Gyann said almost lazily when I started to see black. The trainer circled over to us and laid a hand on the guard's forearm. "Don't break him. We need him. Plus he's technically your superior."

The beast dropped me. Although my vision blurred, I managed to stay upright. I gasped, coughing as I sucked down cold, fresh air.

The trainer plucked the pike from the ground and said gruffly, "Good."

I massaged my throat and glared at him.

Dropping his voice so the others couldn't hear, Gyann said, "You're getting your strength back, and you were always so fast. It's a shame that I lost you to inhabitors' training. Not many can land a blow on Sonam. You could have been great in the real army. You still could be."

I shook my head and swallowed down a laugh. Dizziness made me stagger, but I managed a snarl anyway. "Getting my strength back? I lost. I'm never going to be any good without Faern."

"Don't exaggerate," the master snapped. He tapped his crop against my chest, and anger broke through the numbness inside me. "I trained you in the basics as a child. You had promise fighting physically then, and you'll build up your abilities in time. You're strong and you're fit. You don't need a pet wolf to make you a soldier."

I turned away from him. My hands curled into fists. I wasn't ready to listen to him talk about my wolf. Not when the loss still hit me a thousand times a day, each memory a tiny cut. Gyann grabbed my arm and forced me to face him. His midnight eyes danced with fury. "We're not finished with this session."

I wrenched my arm free. "With Faern, I could have torn your throat out before you could look over your shoulder. That brute's too." When his face went white, I pressed on. "I'm done being a soldier who takes orders. I'm training with you because I need to be able to defend myself. Then I'm getting our powers back. But you're not in control of me."

Gyann didn't try to stop me again as I marched away from the practice grove. I held my chin high, then nearly fell as I caught my foot on the edge of a protruding tree root. Blood filled my mouth as my teeth sank into my lower lip.

Blind. Useless. That's what I was now without Faern. When we'd been bonded, the wolf's keen senses had been mine to command. The air had carried information, scents and distant sounds. I stalked forward, and a thin branch whipped across my face, making me yelp. And I'd been able to see better in the dark.

I knew I'd been rude and not quite fair to the training master. My mood wasn't Gyann's fault, not really. He'd stepped forward when no one else had to give us hope again. He was trying to teach the rebel inhabitors how to fight without the magic we'd depended on. He wasn't an inhabitor and never had been. So while the rest of us struggled with the sudden death of our senses now that the bonds were severed, Gyann carried on as he always had: barking orders, training under the moonlight.

I sighed, pushing branches out of the way as I made my way up the hill that led to the main camp.

Many of the other inhabitors no longer left their tents. The sharp loss of the bondmates they'd trained with over years drove them to seek refuge in their beds. Their eyes had become as dull and lifeless as those belonging to one's in the sleeping death. Most of the masters who had once taught us spell work, meditation, connection, and how to fight using another's body, who had mounted Thim's only resistance, just withered, leaving the surviving students to organize ourselves. The rebel camp was as much a graveyard as it was a base. If the Myeik found us now, I don't know how we'd fight back.

When the bonds broke and I came back from the edge of death myself, at first I'd felt grateful. Faern had been slowly dying for years, and as his inhabitor bondmate, I'd been tied to his lifespan. I hadn't wanted to die at seventeen. While my wolf had grown slow and his teeth had started falling out, I'd never even gotten to call myself an adult. I'd wanted to fight. I'd wanted to live. And with the death of the bond, I got another chance.

But as the days passed, I grew more and more aware of what I'd lost. Everything around me seemed dull and hazy, as if concealed behind a wall of smoke. All my food tasted like sour milk. My sense of smell had faded to nothing. Other than my night vision, my sight was more or less unaffected, but that just meant I had to watch while lifelong friends refused food and company and wasted away like they had nothing left to live for. Worst of all was the feeling of absence at the loss of Faern's constant companionship. It was like one of my organs had been removed and the wound packed with nothing but bitter memories.

And Tashi… I struggled even to think about them without a surge of pain.

Tashi, who was both the cause of my affliction and the only source of hope I had left.

Without Tashi, I'd have followed Faern into the afterlife. And selfishly, sometimes part of me hated them for saving me, because if I'd just died, then I wouldn't have had to face what came after. But another part of me clung to the promise I'd made to them and to the hope of a different sort of life to come.

Before all this, I'd never thought of myself as a coward. Now I wasn't so sure.

By the time I scrambled up the final slope to the camp, my legs were trembling. Despite what Gyann said about my fitness, the time I'd spent in the sleeping death had sapped a lot of my strength. We were attended while in the coma, but no amount of force-feeding could match what we needed.

The camp itself was a silent labyrinth of makeshift tents and tethered mountain ponies. Everyone was either training with Gyann in the moonlit grove or had long since gone to bed. Which was just as well, because I didn't really want to talk to anyone, especially after losing to Sonam. At least I had my own tent, so no one had to watch me brood. Ugyen had pulled some strings. I was too important to their "overall strategic mission" now—whatever that meant—to upset.

I thrust aside the tent's heavy curtains and stumbled inside. Then I splashed water on my face from the basin by the bed. I was too exhausted to bathe properly, and I'd have get up at dawn to train again, so what was the point of cleaning up now?

Someone had turned back my sheets and placed a lotus blossom on my pillow. Something about the flower piqued my anger again, and I tossed it to the floor before climbing into the bed. Special treatment for commanders. I'd spent my life fighting and training. I'd nearly died for the cause, and that hadn't been enough to entitle me to any kind of rank. But falling in love and being loved back by the only person who had any ability to bring our power back—that was enough to earn a position in the rebel command structure. That made me valuable.

I leaned my head back against the pillow and dreamed of wolves.

Originally from Chicago, JULIA EMBER now resides in Edinburgh, Scotland. She spends her days working in the book trade and her nights writing teen fantasy novels. Her hobbies include riding horses, starting far too many craft projects, PokemonGo, and looking after her city-based menagerie of pets with names from Harry Potter. Her travels inspire the fantasy worlds she creates, though she populates them with magic and monsters. She is a bisexual, polyamorous writer and often takes part in events for queer teens.

Julia began her writing career at the age of nine, when her short story about two princesses and their horses won a contest in *Touch* magazine. She has since written several novels for Young Adults.

The Tiger's Watch is her third novel.

UNICORN TRACKS

TRACKS

Julia Ember

After a savage attack drives her from her home, sixteen-year-old Mnemba finds a place in her cousin Tumelo's successful safari business, where she quickly excels as a guide. Surrounding herself with nature and the mystical animals inhabiting the savanna not only allows Mnemba's tracking skills to shine, it helps her hide from the terrible memories that haunt her.

Mnemba is employed to guide Mr. Harving and his daughter, Kara, through the wilderness as they study unicorns. The young women are drawn to each other, despite the fact that Kara is betrothed. During their research, they learn of a conspiracy by a group of poachers to capture the unicorns and exploit their supernatural strength to build a railway. Together, they must find a way to protect the creatures Kara adores while resisting the love they know they can never indulge.

www.harmonyinkpress.com